Chapter One

"How much farther?" The Duke of Whitney stuck his head out of the window and yelled at his coachman.

"Not far now, Your Grace, as long as I don't miss the turning."

"Just do your best, Winters."

Robert Tremaine pulled his head back in, and not for the first time of this journey, let loose a string of oaths. The last thing he wanted to do was to head down to the depths of Hampshire for Christmas. Because his favourite horse had gone lame the day before and there was not a decent riding horse to be hired in London so close to Christmas, he had ended up being driven in his carriage, something he considered fit for elderly gentlemen and maiden aunts. He'd rarely ridden in a carriage since he was a lad, and now he remembered why. To top it all, it was snowing a blizzard. They would be lucky to make Charleton for Christmas, if they made it at all.

He grunted as he tried to ease his long legs into a more comfortable position, and gave up. At over six foot in height, the small confines of the coach offered no comfortable position. At least riding his horse, he was in control. Here he had time to do something he did not want to do. He had time to think.

Truth to tell, Robert was dreading this Christmas, his first at Charleton Court as its master. He had been a duke last Christmas but was still in France, still on the battlefield. His mind drifted back to that dreadful day. His beloved Uncle Francis was dead, as was his cousin Christopher, the rightful Duke. Robert's father had died shortly after his birth and his uncle had taken full responsibility for the family.

He and Christopher were closer than most brothers, closer than he was to his own younger brother. They went to school and Oxford together, and when the time came it was inevitable they would join the same regiment, the Hampshire Dragoons of which Uncle Francis was Colonel in Chief.

Robert smiled as he remembered how he and his cousin seemed to lead charmed lives. They were famous in the regiment for their drinking, high spirits, and 'success with the ladies' as their sergeant-major had said, they had led charmed lives until that awful day. His face froze. It had all happened in a blur, although it seemed as though his memory had stretched time. He could not wipe it from his mind.

They went into the battle with the confidence all soldiers need. No soldier can go into a battle thinking they may die. They go in believing they will come through, and until that day, that had been the case. Many times a bullet had whistled past his head. Several times his quick reflexes had deflected a potentially fatal thrust. Both he and Christopher had a few wounds to boast about, and though they had lost some of their friends, they had never come close to serious injury until that day, the day their luck had finally run out. Christopher and Uncle Francis were dead and it was his fault. Every day he was reminded as someone referred to him as Your Grace. He would never be able to forget, or forgive himself.

The self-loathing and guilt swept over him like acid, and he shifted uneasily in his seat. He closed his eyes, knowing he would see his cousin cut down in front of him. Christopher had yelled his name to warn him of the sword slicing towards his left. He turned and when he finished, turned back to see Christopher lying on the ground. In his determination to protect Robert, he had been unaware of the swordsman at his own back. The wound was deep and Robert had seen enough wounds to know that it was fatal. If he had taken more care, Christopher wouldn't have had to look out for him and would be alive today. All Robert could do was sit with him as his life ebbed away.

"You must tell Father," Christopher whispered as his strength diminished. "Tell him that I loved him. It's funny. I don't believe I ever told the old man that, and that I hope I made him proud." He finished in a whisper.

I would like to thank all the people at Melange Publishing for their support and guidance throughout. Huge thanks also to my lovely son, daughter and daughter-in-law for their encouragement, but especially my husband, my own romantic hero who has made endless cups of tea, listened and motivated me. From skiing to writing and all points beyond and between, he has been there, loving and encouraging me.

His uncle had stood ramrod stiff as Robert told him his only child was dead. "Thank you for telling me, Robert, I appreciate that you were with him when he died. That's a great comfort."

"I'm sorry, Sir."

"I know, Robert."

"It should have been me, uncle."

"You must not think that Robert. You must never think that. We all have a span of time allotted to us, and it was Christopher's time. I should like to be alone now." His voice was low and Robert realised how much his uncle was struggling to retain his control.

His batman woke him and told that his uncle was dead. He had gone out onto the field to see where his son had fallen. His officer's uniform made him an easy target for a French sniper. Robert knew though that he had gone out inviting death. In one night he had lost the only father he had ever known and a cousin he could not have loved better if he had been his brother.

The carriage suddenly swung around jolting him almost off his seat and bringing his thoughts back to the present. "What the hell is happening, Winters?" He stuck his head out the window again.

"I think you should come and see this, Sir."

Robert jumped to the ground, landing softly on the freshly fallen snow. It was already several inches deep and large flakes were still swirling. Winters and a groom were standing some way in front of the horses holding a lantern.

"What is it? A fallen tree?"

"I'm not quite sure, Sir, the horses must have sensed it. They stopped and that's why we skidded."

Robert walked over and bent down. "My God, it's a body."

"Is it dead?" the groom asked.

"I don't know. Bring the lantern closer."

He rolled the body over and his eyes widened. "God in heaven. It's a woman."

"Is she dead? I can't see how she can be alive in this weather," the groom said.

He touched her face. It was pale in the light of the lantern. "I think she's alive. There's only a slight dusting of snow on her so I don't think

3

she's been here long, but she's very cold. We need to get her into the carriage fast and make as much haste as you can, Winters."

"We're on the grand drive, Sir. I'll go as fast as I can. They're good horses, sure footed and brave. It's only a mile, shouldn't be too long, even in this weather."

Robert carried her to the carriage and laid her on the seat, not entirely sure that she was breathing. She was a lady, he knew that from the riding habit and cloak she wore, both of which were damp. He removed the cloak and covered her with his own. She still had not moved. He touched her hand. It felt icy. His cloak was not making a difference.

He had to make a decision. That she was alone with him in a carriage was enough to ruin her reputation whoever she was, but if he left her on the opposite seat he knew she would die. He had seen the dangers of cold on the battlefield with men in uniforms which did not protect them, let alone a slip of a girl in a wet velvet riding habit. His decision made, he hauled her to him and pulled the cloak over them both, willing the heat from his body to bring life back to hers.

The carriage seemed to move in slow motion down the sweeping driveway. It may have been seconds or minutes before the girl in his arms caught her breath and began to shiver.

"That's good. It shows you're alive," he muttered.

She had clearly taken a tumble and banged her head. There was a trickle of blood from her temple. It didn't look too bad, but you could never tell with head injuries. Whether she had other injuries it was difficult to tell in the small confines of the coach. That would have to wait until they were at the house, though it would be impossible to get Doctor Barnes out in this weather. The responsibility for this girl's life lay in his hands.

God knew what the servants would make of this. He idly twirled a silken skein of her hair around his fingers. This is the first time he'd been back as master and he arrived with an unconscious woman. No doubt the story would be told in the servant's hall for years.

He almost groaned as his mind pursued the thought. His mother was also due to arrive at any time for Christmas, along with his younger brother. They had been visiting his sister at her estate in Yorkshire who could not travel as she was about to give birth to the next Earl of

4

Thurnscoe. There was no doubt his mother would make it through the snow. She would definitely arrive despite the blizzard because she was a force of nature on her own. Forceful was how he had heard someone describing her when they had not known he was listening. It was a good word. Battle-axe was the one he might have used.

Ever since he had inherited the title she had been pressing him to marry and have children to secure the inheritance. Having produced one girl and two boys, she had done her duty as a wife and knew the importance of continuing the line. There would be no point inheriting if someone else were to come along and reap the benefit because there was no heir. Everywhere he went, she was there, thrusting blushing virgins at him. To be honest, he had grown to dread meeting her at any social occasion.

The girls were all pretty, he could not deny that. However, half of them seemed to have no thoughts in their heads beyond the next bonnet they were going to buy. They bored him within half an hour. Certainly they were all well-bred and accomplished. They played, they danced, they sang, they sketched. They had been brought up to please, first their fathers and then their husbands. What they hadn't been brought up to do was think, or if they had, they hid it very well.

Now his mother was about to descend on him and he had an unconscious girl to explain.

Chapter Two

The jolt of the carriage as it stopped told Robert they had reached the house. Normally the staff would be lined on the steps to greet him, but there was only Hunter the butler and Mrs. Frazer the housekeeper. The rest of the staff waited in the hall.

"I hope you don't object, Your Grace. It seemed sensible to let the staff wait inside in view of the weather," Hunter said.

"Of course not." Robert was already past him and addressing the housekeeper. "Mrs. Frazer, this woman was injured on the road outside the gates. She needs a warm bath and putting to bed immediately. She's very cold. I think my sister left some of her clothes here last time, so you should find something to fit."

"I'll get the Blue Room ready. It won't take a moment." She turned to give orders to the maids and by the time she had turned back, Robert was halfway up the stairs, carrying the girl.

As he laid her on the bed, two maids were already getting the bath and water was arriving to fill it. Another maid arrived with towels and a fourth brought a nightgown from his sister's room. Mrs. Frazer stood by the bed.

"Perhaps you'd like to get a bite to eat now, Your Grace, and leave this poor young thing to us. We'll take good care of her I promise. What is her name?"

"I have no idea, Mrs. Frazer. When we picked her up, she was barely breathing. Another few minutes and I fear we would have been too late. I'm not sure she's out of the woods yet. She's very cold."

"Then the sooner you leave her to us, the sooner she'll be tucked up in bed. I've sent for warming pans and the fire will soon warm the room."

Robert left. When Mrs. Frazer gave an order in her quiet voice, it was obeyed, from the least important member of staff to the Duke himself. He had seen her in action as a boy and the lesson had not been forgotten.

In the salon, Hunter had already poured a large glass of brandy which Robert thankfully consumed, welcoming the warmth as it hit his throat.

"I see you have a young lady with you, Your Grace." Hunter was the master of understatement. What he really meant was what the hell is going on?

"We found her on the road, just outside the gate. She must have fallen from a horse as she's wearing a riding habit. I think she hit her head. She was unconscious, and had she been there much longer, I fear she would have frozen to death."

"Do you know the young lady, Your Grace?" Hunter poured another brandy.

"I've no idea who she is."

"Most irregular. Will the young lady be staying for Christmas, Sir?"

"I really have no idea, Hunter, I imagine someone must be looking for her, and when they come, she'll go back to wherever it is she came from. Someone is probably missing her and seeking her as we speak." Though as he said it a thought occurred to him, why would a young woman ride out when the conditions were clearly dangerous? Either she was very headstrong, stupid, or afraid of something.

"I will make some enquiries, Sir, regarding the young lady. I merely ask, for as you know, we are to have quite a large house party this festive season. Your honoured mother sent a message to say she had invited some additional guests."

"Hunter, correct me if I'm wrong, but the last time I looked, and I haven't seen them all, there were over a hundred rooms in this house. However many additional guests my mother has invited, I think we can manage to accommodate one more. Who else is she bringing by the way?"

"I believe Lady Arabella Walmsley and her parents will be joining us."

Robert managed to remove all traces of irony from his voice before replying. "How…. nice. We shall be quite a party this year."

He had known and not particularly liked Arabella since she was in leading strings. She had been obnoxious as a child, constantly reminding him he was the poor boy taken in by his uncle. He had not seen her for years but had little reason to believe she had improved.

Although the daughter of an Earl, it was quite clear who ruled the household. There had been talk of her marrying Christopher, but since his death no doubt his mother had marked her out as Duchess material. Arabella would not pass up the opportunity to be addressed as 'Your Grace,' so perhaps her distaste for his lower social position in the past had disappeared and her affections had transferred. He could not really blame her in some ways. Women of their class rarely married for love. If a couple were lucky, they might fall in love after the wedding, but among the ton such marriages were rare.

Hunter poured more brandy and placed a tray with a supper of cold meats, bread, cheese, and fruit in front of him. Robert hadn't realised how hungry he was until his eyes fell on the food. Hunter quietly withdrew.

His reverie was interrupted by Mrs. Frazer who came to report. "The young lady is in bed, Sir. One of the maids will sit with her. She seems warmer, but there's something I think you should see."

"Is she conscious?" he asked as they made their way up the stairs.

"She was barely conscious throughout the whole proceedings, Sir. I am a little worried about the blow to the head. I think there may be a little concussion."

"Is that what concerns you, Mrs. Frazer?" he asked as they entered the room and she nodded to the maid to withdraw.

"Not as much as this, Sir."

The woman was sleeping on her side with her arm thrown around the pillow. Mrs. Frazer leaned forward and pulled the nightgown to reveal her neck and shoulder.

"Good God," Robert exclaimed as he leaned forward. "That's clearly the mark from a…" he met Mrs. Frazer's eye.

"Riding crop, Sir, and there are bruises on her throat."

"Someone has beaten this woman and apparently tried to strangle her. No wonder she was out in this terrible weather. She must have been running away from her attacker."

"Do you think it could have been a highwayman?" she asked.

"I should think even the most hardy highwayman wouldn't venture out on a night like this. Besides, they usually attack on the turnpike roads. It's possible I suppose but there has never been an attack out here."

"Perhaps she was attacked some distance away and was thrown from her horse just outside."

"It's possible, but I still think a highwayman or footpad wouldn't want to be out in the middle of a blizzard."

"I suppose so."

"She's been unconscious for some time now, Mrs. Frazer. Get Winters to fetch Doctor Barnes first thing in the morning. Someone must sit with her through the night."

"Yes, Sir, I'll arrange it."

He looked again at the motionless form. "Who is she?"

"That is a mystery, Sir."

He made a decision. "I'll tell you what, Mrs. Frazer, I know I shall not sleep if I go to bed now so I'll sit with her for a while."

If she was shocked, she did not show it. "Is that quite proper, Sir? A young, unconscious, unmarried woman?"

He smiled. "Trust me, Mrs. Frazer. She spent a good half hour in a carriage with me in a similar state without a chaperone. If that's not enough to ruin a girl's reputation, then I don't know what is. However, we're far from the gossip mongers and scandal makers of London so no-one needs to know. My intentions are quite proper, I assure you, as an officer and a gentleman."

"I'm sure there are many young girls who have fallen for that line, Sir, so I hope you know what you are doing. My girls will be glad of a decent night's sleep what with all the guests this Christmas they've more than enough work to do." She turned towards him at the door. "You be careful with this young woman, Sir. It takes little for a young woman's reputation to be ruined and, once it is gone, she is finished."

He settled into the chair by the side of the bed and looked at the mystery woman, her story was beginning to intrigue him. He knew she was unmarried—there was no ring or mark where one had been removed. A husband who beat his wife was hardly unusual, yet Robert couldn't understand why a man would treat a woman in that way. So, clearly it wasn't a violent husband, of course it could be a jealous lover. He turned the idea over in his mind. It was possible, but so was Mrs. Frazer's suggestion of a robber, and there was the fact that she had nothing with her when she was found.

The woman sighed and turned towards him, her dark lashes fanned almost down to her cheek. He wondered idly what colour her eyes would be; brown he decided, to go with her dark hair. Now that he looked at it by the light of the candle, her hair wasn't just brown. There were lighter and darker strands in it. Tumbled on the pillow, it obscured some of her face and he wanted to see all of it. Instinctively, he leaned forward and pushed the errant locks away. He caught his breath. She was beautiful. Anger rushed through him. He wanted to kill the man who had beaten her. God in heaven, what if her assailant hadn't stopped at the beating?

She stirred again and a small whimper escaped her lips. Her movements became jerky as she turned again. "No, no," she whispered. "Please don't. Let me go... I'll be good."

He knew instantly she was having some kind of nightmare, but it seemed deeper than the nightmares with which he was familiar. She was unable to wake from it. She was now in great distress.

"Shhh, shhh, it's all right. I'm here. I won't let anyone hurt you." He held her hand, but she was not comforted,

"Please, don't...please."

Without giving it a second thought he stretched out beside her and pulled her to him in a tight embrace. At first she fought him, but as he crooned soothingly and stroked her hair she began to relax against him. He listened until he heard her breathing return to its steady rhythm, her head snuggled against his shoulder.

He might have trouble explaining this to the doughty matrons of the ton. Hell, he'd have enough trouble explaining it to Mrs. Frazer, but he was not of a mind to move. For the first time in a long time, he felt relaxed, and soon he too was asleep.

"Your Grace!" The scandalised tones assaulted his ears and he was instantly awake. Mrs. Frazer was leaning over him, taking in the scene. "I knew this would happen," she continued, "You get out of that bed immediately and back to your own room or that poor girl's reputation won't be worth a spit."

He didn't need any second telling. He knew in houses like his, gossip travelled faster than a racehorse. Fortunately, he made it before Hunter appeared with his coffee.

"The weather has improved a little, Your Grace. Winters has taken the sleigh to fetch Dr. Barnes as you instructed. I believe the young lady is still unconscious?"

"If you say so." Robert had been at enough gambling tables to know when to show his hand. "A head injury can be difficult to predict."

"Quite so, Sir. Will Dr. Barnes be staying to luncheon?"

"I imagine so, Hunter, having dragged him from his fireside, the least we can do is feed the man. What time did Winters leave?"

"At first light, Sir. He should be back within the hour."

"Good, after breakfast I'll be in the library. Let me know when Dr. Barnes has seen our patient."

For the next few hours Robert was ensconced at his desk. Now that he had come to terms with his title and the responsibilities he had inherited, he needed to learn quickly if the estates and the people who depended on them were to remain in good order. He said a mental prayer of thanks to his uncle who had made some excellent investments. It would give him time to get to know the details of what he had inherited. He was determined that even though this had been thrust upon him, he would not let his ancestors down.

He was just beginning to feel both stiff from sitting at his desk for so long and hungry, when there was a knock at the door and the figure of Dr. Barnes appeared.

"Your Grace? Hunter said I might find you in here."

"Come in, Doctor. Please, sit down."

He waited a little impatiently while the doctor settled himself in one of the wing chairs and accepted the offered sherry.

"What do you make of the patient? Has she regained consciousness yet? Do you have any idea who she is?"

Dr. Barnes smiled the reassuring smile which made him such a popular physician. "The young lady is still unconscious, and we shall just have to let time do its healing. As you know, a head injury is a serious thing. That she hasn't died already leads me to believe we might have some hope of a recovery, though it is of course difficult to say at this time."

He paused and sipped his sherry. "As to your other questions, Your

11

Grace, I am at as much a loss as you are. She is certainly not local or clearly I would have known her. I would say she is a lady, but who she is and where she came from is a mystery to me. I dare say she will be able to enlighten us herself when she wakes."

"What if she doesn't wake?"

"We'll face that when it happens, though if the young lady's presence here is a problem. I'm sure there would be——"

"Her presence is no problem." Robert spoke more sharply than he intended. "Now, shall you be joining us for luncheon? Hunter assures me that cook has prepared a most excellent sirloin."

"I'm afraid I must decline your kind offer, Your Grace. The journey here was difficult enough, even with Winters in your most excellent sleigh, but I am anxious to return."

"Very well." Robert pulled the cord and waited for Hunter to appear.

"Mrs. Barnes is very much looking forward to the Solstice Ball," Dr. Barnes ventured. "We wondered whether you would keep the tradition going after all that has happened."

Robert forced a smile. "I don't think my mother would ever forgive me if I let that tradition lapse—it's where she met my father."

"Nor any of the other ladies of the parish I surmise." Dr. Barnes chuckled. "It's where many a romance began."

Dr. Barnes had not long gone when Hunter tapped once more on the library door. "I beg your pardon for interrupting, Your Grace, but Winters requests a word with you."

"Winters?" Robert was intrigued. His years in the army had made sure he could get on with any man, no matter what their rank might be, but Winters was both a man of few words and uncomfortable unless he was either sitting on a horse or talking about one.

"Bring him in without delay."

As he expected, Winters was most uncomfortable. He stood on the carpet looking as though he hoped a hole would open up and swallow him. He twisted his hat around in his hands, holding on to it as though his life depended on it.

"What is it, Winters? Is there something wrong with the horses?" Robert encouraged him.

"No, Your Grace, your horses are fine. It's about that young lady,

Sir."

Robert was instantly alert. "What about her?"

"Well. I think I found her horse. When I came back with the doctor I saw a horse among the trees, a hunter my Lord and a fine bred one with an expensive lady's saddle. Cold like that young lady, but it must have had enough shelter in the trees. I brought him back, rubbed him down, and he's in the stable."

"And the horse seems well? No ill-effects from being out?"

"No, Sir, he was hungry mind, but we fed and watered him and now he's warm in the stable, a fine beast, Your Grace. He'll need exercising in a day or so. I don't think he's used to standing around."

"Then get one of the stable hands to take him out as you see fit."

"What about the young lady, Sir?" Winters voice failed.

"Dr. Barnes says we must allow time to take its course. In the meanwhile, Winters, take care of her horse. She will no doubt want to ride when she is well enough."

"Very good, Your Grace." Winters bowed and left. Robert could almost feel his relief.

Sitting at his desk, Robert eyed the papers in front of him, though his mind was on the young woman upstairs. For some reason he could not name, it had become vital to him that she should get well. He could not save his uncle or his cousin, but he would damn well save her.

His reverie was interrupted by the library door being flung open by his mother. Lady Helen Tremaine followed social custom if it suited her and flouted it if it did not. She did not care to wait for Hunter so she sought her son by herself.

"Robert darling, I thought I should never get here, the journey has been positively hideous and it's snowing again. I swear we shall have another foot of it by Christmas. Your sister sends her love and wishes she could join us but is too near her time to be travelling half-way across the country. Your brother will be here in the next day or so. What is this I hear about some stray waif you picked up off the road?"

"Good afternoon, Mother. I wondered whether you might decide to stay with Sophie for Christmas. The 'stray waif' you mention is a young woman we literally found in the road. We don't know who she is, but hopefully she will wake up soon and we shall be able to return her to her family."

His mother raised a perfectly arched eyebrow. "How very curious. What sort of young woman would be out without a chaperone? I'm not sure that I approve Robert. This could be very damaging to your reputation."

"What did you expect me to do mother? Leave her to die of cold outside my gate? I doubt that would have enhanced my reputation." He loved his mother, but she could irritate him like no other person.

"Of course not, but there are other places. You have no idea who this young woman is, surely—"

"Mother, there are times when you appear to be an appalling snob."

"Really, Robert, that is most hurtful, I have always done my duty for the poor."

"As long as they know their place."

"I fear we are getting off on the wrong foot, Robert. I truly don't want to fight with you, I know sometimes the things I say rile you, but I know how society works, my son. If this mysterious girl is a member of the ton, her reputation will be compromised by her being here with you, however innocent it may be in reality. It may already be the case that she is already unmarriageable because of your good deed."

"If society is really that shallow then I want nothing more to do with it. If necessary, I'll marry her myself. That will give the gossips something to talk about." Robert was disgusted with the hypocrisy with which judgements were made and his own motives, which, he had to admit, were not quite as pure as he would like.

"Don't be ridiculous, darling. You have a duty to continue the family line and to do that you need society. Arabella and her parents will be joining us for the holiday. The Earl is re-building, the castle is in uproar, and his town house is unfinished, so I suggested they might come here. We have plenty of rooms, and Arabella has grown into a handsome young woman."

"Mother, you are so transparent."

"Arabella would make a marvellous Duchess. She has been brought up for it. She is beautiful, accomplished, and knows how society works. Just think about it, dear. Spend some time and get to know her. Now, ring for Hunter to bring some tea."

Chapter Three

His mother was going to be impossible. He should have known there was no subject on which she didn't have an opinion, regardless of whether she actually knew anything about it. The rooms were too cold, the furniture was placed in the wrong position, the maids' dresses were the wrong colour. Robert needed new clothes and could not wander around in his old army uniform if he wanted to be part of fashionable society. He did not.

He was relieved when she retired to bed with a headache. Before he settled down in the library for a final glass of brandy, he decided to stop by the Blue Room. Mrs. Frazer was sitting with his guest.

"No change?"

"I think she's breathing easier and the nightmares don't seem so intense, so maybe she's coming around a bit."

"Who is she?" he murmured,

"I'm sure we'll find out very soon."

He had barely poured his drink in his library when one of the maids knocked on the door. "Mrs. Frazer said to come straightaway, Your Grace," she stammered before she fled.

Curious, Robert hurried to the Blue Room.

"She opened her eyes twice, fleetingly, but definitely open." Mrs. Frazer looked relieved. "I think she's coming back to us."

As she spoke, the figure on the bed opened her eyes, and with a sharp intake of breath, glanced around the room. Her eyes widened and Robert could almost feel her fear. He didn't miss the glance at the door.

15

"It's all right," he began, "you're—"

She was out of bed but took only three steps before she crumpled. Fortunately, his legendary reflexes had not deserted him. She was fast, remarkably so for a woman who had been unconscious for twenty-four hours, but he was faster. He gathered her to him. She was slight, but there was no doubting that she was a woman, and, he noted with some alarm, no doubting either the effect she had on him.

He dumped her unceremoniously on the bed. "Now stay there and don't move. You're perfectly safe unless you try that trick again, and I swear I'll put you across my knee. I am Robert Tremaine and this is my housekeeper, Mrs. Frazer."

"Hush, Sir, can't you see you're frightening the poor girl," Mrs. Frazer interrupted him. "Now dear, you just stay there and rest. I'm going to see to some tea. You must be famished. I'll leave you in the charge of Alice and His Grace here, who will no doubt be the perfect gentleman and not shout or threaten you." As she spoke, Mrs. Frazer deftly tucked the covers and patted the girl's shoulder and, with a warning glance at Robert, she left the room, pausing at the door. "Shall I send for Doctor Barnes?"

Robert considered the matter. "No, we'll wait until morning when travelling will be safer. The last thing we need is another accident."

The girl's eyes followed Mrs. Frazer's retreating form then transferred to Robert. Her eyes were green, like polished emeralds. Now he knew.

"Where am I? What is this place?" Her voice was low and slightly husky.

"You're at my home, Charleton Court. You had an accident and have been unconscious. We found you in the road outside. If we hadn't found you when we did, you wouldn't have survived. You were frozen."

"Why was I there?"

"I have no idea. I was hoping you would be able to give me the answer to that question, Miss?"

"I…don't know." She paused before her emerald eyes focused on him, and he saw the fear in them. "I don't know my name… I don't know who I am. I don't remember anything before I opened my eyes a few moments ago."

Her hand went to her mouth as she tried to stifle the tears that threatened to overwhelm her. Robert recognised courage when he saw it. There was the raw physical courage he had witnessed many times on the battlefield, and he knew women needed courage to face the dangers of childbirth, but this woman showed courage in not wanting to appear weak, even though she faced the terrifying prospect of not knowing her own identity. He acted instinctively as he had done since the moment he had plucked her from the snow. Somehow he knew he had to protect her. He wanted to protect her. He sat on the bed and gathered her to him.

"It will be fine. You had quite a blow to the head, so loss of memory is not unusual. After a few days' rest, things will be clearer. I've seen it before. The important thing is not to worry about it.

She looked up at him with hope and trust. "Do you really think so?"

"I really do." He smiled down at her. There was a moment when he knew that if she made just the slightest move towards him, he would kiss her. He was filled with disgust at himself.

What was he doing? His conscience protested. He was about to take advantage of a helpless woman who did not even know who she was or why she was lying in the snow. What sort of a man was he?

Robert quickly released her, but not before he traced his fingers across her cheek. It felt as soft as he imagined. He stood up quickly and stalked to the fireplace, deciding that a little distance between them would be a good idea. He might then be able to think straight.

"Perhaps we should think of a name for you to use temporarily until you get your memory back?" he suggested, trying to lighten the tension that had come on the room. "I can't carry on calling you 'the girl,' can I?"

"I suppose not."

"Then what would you like your temporary name to be? Gertrude? Clara? Fanny?" He grinned as she wrinkled her delicate nose in disgust at his suggestions. "How about Josephine? Beryl? Ruby?"

She rolled her eyes.

"Winnifred? Ethelberga?" He was rewarded with a weak giggle.

"Can I help it if your taste in names is bizarre, if not say truly appalling?"

"Then help me. It seems I have been doing all the work. You who have the most to gain from this exercise, I might add, have not made a single suggestion."

"Very well, how about Jane?"

He tilted his head to take in the finely arched eyebrows, retroussé nose, full lips, and the delicate features framed by a riot of chestnut curls. "No, you do not strike me as a Jane."

"Joan then?"

He shook his head.

"Penelope?"

"Definitely not."

"Harriet?"

"Now you're being perverse."

"Emma?" As she said the word, he noticed her eyes darken.

"What is it? Do you remember something? What do you remember?" He was at her side.

She paused before sighing. "I don't know. I just had a feeling, a glimpse of something. It was blurred and far away and over so quickly, I could have imagined it."

"No, I doubt it. Emma clearly means something to you."

"But what if I never remember who I am?" Her voice shook.

He took her hand. "You will." He spoke with a confidence he did not entirely feel. "If for some reason you don't, we shall have to make a life for you. Now for a surname. I think perhaps something that is easily remembered, though I think, under the circumstances I may refer to you by the name Emma in the hope that it jogs your memory in some way. My mother will, of course, not approve, but we shall cross that bridge when we come to it."

Their conversation was interrupted by the arrival of Mrs. Frazer with a tray. She quickly shooed Robert from the room and insisted that whatever they needed to discuss could be done in the morning.

He grinned. "Good night, Miss Emma."

"Good night."

He was rewarded with a smile.

Chapter Four

Emma woke up feeling refreshed, for the first time in what seemed a lifetime. There were no nightmares, and the pain in her head had receded to a dull ache. Her eyes scanned the room looking for something to orient herself. Then, she remembered the conversation of the previous evening which had taken on a dream like quality.

She went through the story her rescuer had told her, hoping to trigger a memory, something, anything, but there was just a blank. Sighing, she got out of bed and went to the window. She could either give in to the fear lurking at the edges of her mind or she could try and be positive in the hope her memory would return and she could go back to her real life. One thing was certain. She did not want to mope around in bed. She had been inactive for long enough and needed some fresh air.

As she pulled back the heavy drapes, she gasped at the sight of the snow covered landscape. Below her was a fountain, frozen in time. The snow had covered every feature in the formal garden, which she knew must be close to the house, right through the park, and into the distant horizon. It was a fresh, white world; quite magical. She could not wait to go outside.

She was still taking it in when the door opened, and Alice came in carrying several gowns. "Oh, you're awake, Miss. My name is Alice and Mrs. Frazer sent me to be your maid while you're here. But you shouldn't be out of bed. I must fetch Mrs. Frazer at once."

"Please don't, Alice. I'm really feeling much better."

"But I have to let Mrs. Frazer know the minute you are awake and she is to call Doctor Barnes. His Grace was most insistent." Alice looked worried.

"Alice, I promise you I am feeling fine, I would really like to get dressed. Why don't we give His Grace a surprise?"

"Are you sure, Miss, because I don't want to get into trouble."

"I promise you won't get into trouble, Alice. If anyone is to get into trouble it will be me. What do you have there?" Emma nodded at the armful of beautiful fabrics Alice was clutching.

"His Grace had some of his sister's gowns made to fit if you're ready to dress. Which one would you like to wear?" Alice had clearly given up, recognising that Emma was determined.

"Oh I really don't mind, Alice, whichever you think." Emma smiled, she had learned something about herself already. She didn't really care about gowns since there were other things to think and do.

"Well, Miss, I think the green will suit your colouring and there are matching slippers that Miss Sophie outgrew."

Before she knew it, Alice had organised her bath and tamed her curls into something of style and the dress and slippers fitted her perfectly. As she examined her reflection in the looking glass, a thought occurred to her.

"Thank you, I don't think my hair is very easy to tame. Alice, do you think you could find some breeches and boots so that I can go out. The gown is lovely, but I want some fresh air and it's hardly suitable for the snow. I promise you won't get into trouble," she added. "I'll pretend I found them when I was exploring one of the rooms."

Alice could not have looked more shocked if Emma had asked to dress as a pirate, but she suddenly grinned conspiratorially at her temporary mistress. "I think I know where I can find something, Miss. I'll take you down to the dining room for breakfast. His Grace will get a surprise. While you're eating I'll find them out. You're sure I won't get into trouble?"

Emma grinned back and nodded. "You have my solemn promise."

Alice set off at a trot and Emma had no option but to follow.

Robert was drinking coffee when she entered.

"Good Morning, Your Grace," she said breezily and curtseyed.

He choked. "What the devil? What are you doing out of bed?"

"I am perfectly fine, my lord, apart from a slight headache which is not improved by your shouting."

"I am not shouting," he responded.

"No, Sir? I imagine they heard you in the kitchen."

"You should be in bed," he continued in a lower tone. "You have had an accident and a head injury. You should not be moving about at least until the doctor has seen you."

"I feel perfectly well. I don't have a fever and I am sure that is what the doctor would say."

"Do you remember anything?"

Her smile faded. "I'm afraid not, Sir, but I'm sure I shall very soon."

"I am so glad you do not seem to have acquired the habit of many young girls of lolling about in bed for half the morning," Lady Tremaine announced as Emma sat down. "I do not approve of laziness in any form. People, especially young people, need employment of some sort or they begin to make mischief. I hope you do not intend any mischief. Miss...?"

"We have decided on the name Smith until Emma's real name emerges," Robert improvised.

"Really, Robert, surely you could have been a little more imaginative. Smith is hardly an appropriate name for a lady."

Emma rose and curtseyed. "Hopefully it won't be too long before I remember my own name, Your Grace, or someone comes looking for me," she added softly, wondering why no-one apparently seemed to be missing her.

Robert rose and stalked to the door. "I have business with the estate manager and will send for Barnes. Mother, try not to intimidate Miss Smith."

Both Emma and Lady Tremaine watched him go. Noticing the direction of Emma's gaze, his mother continued. "I am not Your Grace. Robert's father was the younger son. You may address me as Your Ladyship. My father was the Earl of Burton."

"Thank you, Your Ladyship."

"Well you certainly seem to have been brought up with the manners of a lady," Lady Tremaine conceded.

"You are kind, Your Ladyship." Emma replaced her tea cup and reached for some toast.

"Though for a lady, you certainly seem to have a remarkably healthy appetite."

Emma paused as she momentarily considered not eating, but she discovered two further things about herself. Firstly, she was very hungry and secondly, she was not entirely in awe of Lady Tremaine.

"Robert has, of course, had to make several adjustments since inheriting the title so suddenly and unexpectedly. His uncle and cousin died within hours of each other."

"I am sorry. I had no idea." Emma was shocked and saddened. She knew how it felt to be alone. It wasn't a memory, but it was something.

"Of course," Lady Tremaine continued, "Now that Robert has inherited, he must settle the question of an heir. It is vitally important he marry someone suitable—someone who will be able to support him as he takes his place at the forefront of society."

"Of course," Emma replied. It was obvious Lady Tremaine expected some kind of response and she had not missed the stress on the word suitable.

"Fortunately, Robert knows his duty, and I think I can confidently say that by Old Year's Night a betrothal will be announced."

"How nice," Emma responded wondering why his mother was going into the details of the Duke's private life.

"Yes, Lady Arabella Walmesly will be arriving today. Robert and she have known each other since childhood. She is a wonderful choice—well bred, cultured, and accomplished. She will make the perfect Duchess."

"His Grace will be a lucky man." Emma picked at her table napkin, wondering how quickly she could make her escape.

Lady Tremaine's eyes narrowed. "Now we come to you my dear. What are we to do with you?"

Emma looked up. "I'm not quite sure what your ladyship means."

The older woman smiled, but it did not reach her eyes. She took a deep breath. "What I am about to say Miss Smith may appear to be indelicate, but I'm afraid delicacy must be sacrificed in the interests of clarity." Emma returned her look steadily without speaking. "In fact, my son and Lady Arabella are to be betrothed and nothing is to disrupt it."

"I understand."

"I don't wish to be unkind, my dear, but it is as well to nip any unsuitable ideas in the bud. Do not set your cap at my son, Miss Smith. He will marry Lady Arabella who is his social equal. You, however, are not. Now, my son may have taken pity on you in this most unfortunate and unusual circumstance, but I must warn you not to mistake kindness and charity for attachment. I hope I have made your position clear."

Emma learned another element of her personality during that speech. "Perfectly, Your Ladyship, but if the betrothal is so certain I wonder why you feel the need to warn me off. It would suggest either your son or the young lady is less than constant. For my own part, I hardly know His Grace. He has shown me nothing but kindness and respect, which is more, if I may say then you. I assure Your Ladyship I shall leave as soon as possible. Now, if you will excuse me?" Emma gave the briefest of curtseys and was out of the room, leaving Lady Tremaine open mouthed.

Emma ran up the stairs with her thoughts in a whirl. How dare that woman suggest she wasn't good enough? Well she hoped Lady Arabella, whoever she was, had plenty of spirit. She would need it.

Alice had returned and was laying clothes on the bed. "I found these, Miss. We had a stable lad in the summer, Jack, but he left. Anyway, here's his clothes. They're a bit big, but I think they'll do."

"Why did he leave?" Emma struggled out of her gown and into the breeches.

"Turns out his mother was more high born than anyone knew, and when her husband died, his grandfather sent for her and Jack, 'cos he had no other children. So it turns out Jack is his heir. It's a nice story isn't it, Miss? Like a fairy tale."

"Not every rich family is a happy one, Alice." Emma stood perfectly still for a moment. Where had that thought come from?

"Are you all right, Miss? You've gone very pale. Should I fetch Mrs. Frazer?" Alice looked concerned.

"No, thank you. I'll be fine." Emma shook her head as if to dislodge the unease she felt. "How do I look?" he asked, tucking her hair firmly into the cap.

"Oh, Miss, even your own mother wouldn't recognise you."

"Now let me see if I agree." She turned to the cheval mirror where a cheeky urchin grinned back. "You're right Alice. Let's hope the Duke doesn't either."

Chapter Five

"You lad, wait."

Emma froze and pulled the cap lower as she turned and said, "Yes, ma'am?"

The cook held out a large basket. "Take this lot to Mr. Winters in the stable and be quick about it. He likes his bread warm does Mr. Winters."

"Yes, Ma'am."

"And wipe your feet when you come back for his dinner. I don't want no slushy boots dirtying my kitchen."

"Yes, Ma'am," Emma repeated.

"Well, what are you waiting for?"

Emma needed no second bidding. She grasped the basket and was out of the door.

"I swear those stable lads get scrawnier," the cook muttered.

Outside, the cold hit Emma and she shivered, aware of how thin her borrowed clothes were. A path had been cleared, she assumed to the stables, so she set off to follow it. Her guess was right. It trailed farther down the sweeping drive but to her left she saw the handsome stables. In a few moments she was pushing open the door.

"Come here, lad, set the basket down yonder, and shut the door."

It took a second for Emma's eyes to adjust from the brightness of the snow outside to the dimmer light when the door was closed. The man she assumed to be Winters was rubbing down a chestnut hunter, who seemed skittish.

"Over here, lad, and hold his bridle." Winters turned back to the horse, speaking softly. "I'll not be hurting thee, lad."

Emma could scarcely breathe. "Apollo," she murmured softly. "His name is Apollo." She took his bridle and there was a moment when the horse hesitated, stopped prancing, and stood still. His face nuzzled her neck.

"I'll be damned." Winters stepped back. "Yon horse belongs to that young lady as was injured, but he seems to have taken to you." His eyes narrowed. "Who are you boy, the new kitchen lad? Because you look like you know something about horses. I could do with a lad who's reliable. Good prospects too. Likes his horses does his Grace, likes 'em well looked after. Anyone can be a kitchen boy, but you have to be born to work with horses."

Robert raised an eyebrow, he had never, in all his life heard Winters speak for so long. Both Winters and whoever he was speaking to were so absorbed in their conversation they had not heard him enter the stable. He craned his neck to see and his eyebrows nearly shot off his forehead when he recognised the owner of the other voice.

"I'd like to learn more about horses, especially how to take care of them."

"That's settled then," Winters replied. "I'll have a word with Mrs. Jones and tell her to get a new kitchen lad. She'll complain like the devil…"

"What's this, Winters? We can't have you upsetting Mrs. Jones. Poaching her kitchen lad will mean neither of us gets our dinner. Wait in the tack room, lad, while I speak with Winters."

"Sorry, Your Grace, I didn't mean to overstep the mark." Emma heard Winters say as she sidled out, staying as much in the shadows as she could.

Perhaps the Duke hadn't recognised her. She bobbed a quick bow and tugged her cap, feeling Robert's eyes on her as she passed him.

She stood in the tack room—the smell of leather and horses soothed her a little. How was she going to get through a conversation with Robert? Suddenly her little adventure seemed a little hare-brained. Yet she was also excited, about her horse. Apollo was hers. She had a memory of flying over fences and feeling free. Not only had she recognised Apollo, but she was sure the horse had recognised her as well.

"Well, lad," Robert said as he entered. "Winters, who doesn't impress easily, was impressed by you. Thinks he could train you up to be a coachman. What do you say to that? What's your name, lad?"

Emma thought frantically. "Tom, my Lord, Your Grace, Sir. Mr. Winters is very generous, Sir." Not knowing what to do, she bowed and tugged her cap again.

Robert grinned, enjoying himself. "Now, Tom, if you're to work for me, you need to learn how to behave when the lords and ladies are here. So stand up straight and take your cap off."

"My cap, Sir?"

"Yes Tom, your cap. Take it off."

"What? Now, Sir?"

"I am your employer. I am a Duke, so yes, young man, now."

"I would rather not, Sir, Your Grace." Emma persisted, keeping her eyes firmly on the ground.

"And why not?"

"Lice. Sir," she improvised.

Robert's lips twitched, "Lice?"

"Yes, Sir, all over my head, Sir, something terrible, Sir. If I take my cap off they might get onto you, my lord Duke, Sir."

"You have been impertinent long enough, young Tom."

"But what about the—"

"I survived the battlefield. I believe I'll survive a few lice," Robert replied drily, and before she could stop him, he swept the cap from her head, releasing a sea of chestnut brown curls which fell like a waterfall down her back. Her eyes shot to his. Definitely emeralds of the finest cut he noted absently…

His shoulders rocked, and he raised a hand to his mouth, then looked at her in alarm. Emma blanched white with shock. She stepped back and wrapped her arms around her body in defence, her eyes wide with fear.

"Emma, what's the matter?" Robert spoke quietly.

"You looked like… you were going to…" she stammered.

"You thought I was going to strike you?"

He was shocked. He took a step towards her and she took a step back. He ran his fingers through his hair, remembering the bruising and weals Mrs. Frazer had pointed out to him. Someone had beaten Emma severely, and he suspected, more than once. He was appalled.

He knew fathers beat their children and men beat their wives, though he could not understand why anyone who loved someone, be it child or wife, would want to hurt them. He was also conscious of wanting to kill the insensitive bastard who had done this to Emma.

Robert wanted to take her in his arms and comfort her. He wanted to kiss her until she forgot all her fears, until she forgot everything but him. He wanted her.

"Emma, look at me," he spoke softly. She looked terrified, and he didn't want to frighten her further. She slowly raised her eyes to his. "I promise you, I have never hit a woman and I never will." He moved slowly towards her as he spoke. "I would never harm you, Emma, I swear." He gently prised her arms from her body and drew her into his. "You're trembling." He drew her closer and stroked her hair, trying to soothe her any way he could.

"He hit me with his riding crop." Her voice was faint. "He wanted me to do something and I wouldn't, so he hit me with his hands and his riding crop. He said he would beat obedience into me."

Robert lifted her chin gently with his finger forcing her to look at him "Who, Emma? Who did this to you?"

Her eyes filled with tears. "That's the worst part. I don't know. I don't know who he was and I don't know why he did it. I must have done something terrible for him to treat me so."

"No, Emma, you must not think that." He was horrified, "Nothing you could have done would ever justify that. You must never blame yourself. A real man doesn't need to beat women." Though, he had to concede, if that man was in front of him now, Robert would not be responsible for the damage he would do.

"I kept saying 'please don't,' but he just kept on as though he couldn't hear me… He just kept on…." she sobbed.

Robert gathered her close. "I promise you, Emma, you will never have to face that again, I'll take care of you,"

As soon as the words were out, he knew that was what he wanted to do. It was like a thunderbolt, the *coup de foudre* the French talked about. He didn't just want to take care of her, he wanted all of her. He wanted her in his arms and in his bed. He wanted to hear her cry his name.

At that moment he wanted to kiss away the hurt and pain. He wanted to mold her body to his. He could feel the outline of her breasts against his chest and her thighs against his. She was driving him mad.

He sighed. Emma clearly had little experience of men, and the man who had abused her had been a brute. If Robert was to win her, he must proceed slowly without causing her further fear.

Her sobs were subsiding and she stepped out of his arms. "I'm sorry, Your Grace," she apologised. Her thoughts were in confusion. The memories were painful, but being in his arms had given her feelings she had never experienced before. She felt breathless and dizzy.

"I think we should perhaps have a breath of fresh air," Robert suggested. Now that there was some distance between them, he could begin to think straight. "Put your cap back on and we'll walk." He offered her his arm.

"I can hardly take that, Sir, I am supposed to be a boy." She smiled at him.

"Good point," he grinned back, "but I must observe you are the most unconvincing boy I have ever met."

They walked in companionable silence through the formal garden. The trees and bushes were laden with snow, sparkling in the weak winter sun. Robert pointed out some of the features that would be revealed when the snow melted. They were both charmed to see a robin perching on the bough of a young sapling. It looked curiously at them until they got too close and it then flew off, complaining.

Emma giggled. "He seemed a little upset that we were encroaching on his territory."

Robert smiled "He's probably gone to complain to the landlord."

"That's you." Emma giggled again.

"I shall have to ask him to deal with my estate manager. I have enough trouble dealing with the human tenants without the wildlife complaining as well." The conversation was nonsense, but Emma was smiling and some of the tension had gone from her face.

"What was your favourite place here as a boy, Your Grace?" she asked.

"I'll show you if you will stop calling me Your Grace and use my given name. It's Robert."

"I don't think so, Your Grace. I am aware that our stations in life are vastly different. You are a duke and I am… a stable lad." She laughed, hitting him squarely in the chest with a snowball she had fashioned while he was looking at the robin.

"Why you little—"

She was off, careering through the bushes, dodging, and weaving as he chased after her laughing. Their exchange of snowballs was fairly even, though Emma proved to be a better shot than he, and Robert was not about to let that record stand. He saw her hiding behind a small holly bush. Her back was towards him as she made more ammunition. Stealthily, he crept up behind her and shook the branches causing snow to cascade down onto her head.

Emma shrieked as it found its way down her back, the cold taking her breath away. "Oh, Sir,' she gasped, "that was not the action of a gentleman."

"I may be a duke, but I never said I was a gentleman." He laughed, enjoying himself immensely.

The cold and exercise put colour in Emma's cheeks. Her eyes sparkled and her lips were full and ripe. He reached out a finger and drew the outline of her mouth. His eyes caught hers and held them. Emma could not look away. She licked her lips and he was lost.

Slowly he drew her to him and kissed her gently, savouring the feel of her lips under his. It was not enough, not nearly enough. His arms went around her, and when she opened her mouth to him, passion took over both of them. He explored her mouth with his tongue as he wanted to explore the rest of her body. God, he wanted her. Her arms had slid around his neck and she clung to him.

He would have stayed there forever kissing her. He wanted to brand her so no other man's kiss would move her. The thought of another man kissing her filled him with what he recognised as jealousy and he pulled her closer so she could feel the affect she had on him. Somewhere in the rational part of his brain he heard and registered the sound of the horn, which meant that a carriage was approaching from the gatehouse.

He stepped back. "There's a carriage coming up the drive. Go back to the house through the kitchen. You must not be seen alone with me."

Emma looked at him in confusion. How could someone kiss like that and dismiss her so quickly? Not trusting herself to speak, she nodded and turned away quickly so he would not see her tears.

Robert strode back to the house, his conscience berating him soundly for taking advantage of a young woman he had promised to protect. He should not have kissed her or put his arms around her. In his future dealings with her he would be like a brother to her. It would probably kill him. He turned to welcome Lady Arabella and her parents to his home.

As Emma walked, her thoughts were a jumble. She had no right to hope for anything from Robert Tremaine. He was a duke and she was, well she wasn't sure what she was, but his mother had made it perfectly clear he was way above her station and was practically engaged. Yet if that was so, why had he kissed her? Her breath caught, her lips felt swollen from his sensuous onslaught. Surely anyone who saw her would know she had just been soundly kissed. Emma had been kissed before, she noted, but nothing like that.

Emma crept through the kitchen and managed to find her way back to her room. Somehow she managed to respond to Alice's chat as she helped her to dress.

Chapter Six

Robert turned to greet his guests as the carriage rolled to a halt.

Countess Walmesly took his proffered hand. "So kind of you to invite us, Your Grace. Unfortunately, the castle was in no fit state for anything due to the renovations. Still, one has to be patient in order to get nothing but the best."

"Of course."

"Good of you to have us over the festive season, Your Grace." Lord Walmsley paused to take a pinch of snuff. "This renovation of the old seat is taking a long time and costing a fortune, but you know what Arabella's like when she gets an idea into her head."

"No, Papa, one never receives the best if one settles for less." Lady Arabella followed him from the carriage and held out her hand for Robert to kiss.

She had grown up to be an acknowledged beauty, her fair hair, pale skin, and vivid blue eyes gave her a dramatic appeal, but Robert also saw a hardness in the set of her mouth and her smile did not reach her eyes.

"Sorry to hear of the death of your uncle and poor Christopher. Still it's an ill wind and all that," the Earl went on totally oblivious to the insensitivity of his comments.

Though as a second son, he had inherited unexpectedly so his comments were perhaps more of an indication of his own situation. Robert smiled a tight smile and gestured for him to enter the house. Inwardly he sighed. It was going to be a long Christmas.

As his guests assembled for dinner, he was aware Emma was missing.

Striding to the door, he saw Alice scurrying up the staircase.

"Where is Miss Smith? Is she unwell?" he demanded.

"Please, Your Grace, Miss Smith has a headache and asks you to excuse her this evening," Alice replied as she bobbed a curtsey.

"A headache? When did this come on?" It could be from her injury or something to do with the way they had parted earlier.

"Miss said it came on when she came back from outside. But..." Alice stopped abruptly and flushed bright red, aware she had been about to go too far.

"But?" Robert wasn't about to let her go without hearing what she thought.

"I'm sorry, Your Grace, but it's not my place to say."

"I am prepared to overlook your part in the charade Miss Smith played this morning on the grounds that you are young and Miss Smith is most persuasive, but I want you to tell me what you were about to say. Do it now or my patience will be sorely tested."

"Yes, Sir, sorry, Sir. I was about to say Miss Smith went out in good spirits and when she came back she seemed upset and has been for the rest of the day. Just quiet and thoughtful."

"Thank you. Now I want you to go to Miss Smith and tell her that I expect her to be down here in ten minutes ready to be introduced to my guests." Robert instinctively knew if he allowed Emma to hide away now, she would lose confidence. Losing her memory was difficult enough.

"Yes, Sir."

Alice was half way up the stairs when he added, "And if she argues, tell her I shall come up and carry her if necessary."

"Yes, Sir." He couldn't swear to it, but he was sure Alice was grinning.

* * * *

"He said he would what?" Emma was furious.

"Carry you down, Miss. I think his Grace thought some company would do you good." Alice deftly fastened Emma into her gown.

"Did he indeed?" Emma muttered mutinously.

"There you are, Miss. Pretty as a picture. Now you're ready to meet Lady Arabella."

Ten minutes later a breathless Emma entered the room and glared at Robert.

He met her with a smile. "Ah, Miss Smith, come and meet our other guests." He led her to the sofa where his mother, Lady Arabella, and her mother sat gossiping.

Lady Tremaine glanced up. "Ah, here is the young woman I was telling you about. We are quite intrigued as to who she is. Robert has named her Miss Emma Smith."

Lady Arabella turned her gaze to Emma. "How interesting, Robert. What made you decide on such a tedious name?" she drawled.

"We chose it together, my Lady. Some of the names his Grace suggested were a little unpronounceable," Emma replied. She was not going to allow a conversation to take place about her while she was still there.

"And has no one come forward to claim you yet?" Lady Arabella raised an eyebrow, making it perfectly clear that she thought Emma was in some way malingering in Robert's home.

"Not yet," Robert interjected. "The snow may have delayed matters. Now shall we go into dinner and afterwards perhaps Arabella and Miss Smith will entertain us with some music. Perhaps, Walmesly, you would escort my mother and your wife into dinner and I shall escort Lady Arabella and Miss Smith." He held out his arm to both women.

Arabella, Emma noticed, looked as though she had swallowed a lemon.

Dinner passed slowly. The three ladies conversed about people they knew, the latest fashions, and London gossip, all of which had the effect of excluding Emma from the conversation and sending her a not so subtle message, 'you are not one of us.' Not that Emma minded. She found their conversation less interesting than the one Robert was having with Lord Walmsely on the matter of trade now that the war with France was over. Robert's eyes gleamed as he discussed the matters of land with the older man, who for all his bluster and lack of subtlety held his own in the debate. What became apparent to Emma was Robert's determination to modernise the running of his estate for it to profit, not just for himself, but the workers for whom he felt responsible.

All too soon, the moment Emma had been dreading approached. The women were to withdraw and leave the men to their port. As soon as the ladies were settled, Lady Tremaine announced how much she was looking forward to hearing Arabella perform at the pianoforte because Arabella was quite the most accomplished young lady of her season. This was the first verse in a long litany of Lady Arabella's accomplishments. She danced like an angel, her drawing was superb, her singing quite sublime.

Arabella listened with apparent modesty, interjecting from time to time with "Oh, you go too far."

"Of course, we have no idea what Miss Smith's accomplishments may be, for if she has any, she has forgotten them," Lady Tremaine said, much to the amusement of the two other women.

Emma's face froze into a smile before she picked up a book and began to leaf through it so that she did not have to be a further part of the conversation.

"Look at that," Lady Arabella whispered. "I doubt she can even read. She's holding the book upside down."

In her humiliation, she had picked up the book and was unaware of what was on the pages. She put the book down, intending to excuse herself and go to her room when Robert and the Earl returned.

"You were very quick this evening," his mother observed.

"We were looking forward to hearing the young ladies perform," the Earl responded, settling himself in a chair by the fire.

Arabella jumped up at once. "Of course, Papa, I should be obliged, my dear Whitney, if you would turn the pages for me."

Robert nodded and followed her to the pianoforte. Emma watched as he helped her find the music and settled her on the stool, sitting close so that he could turn the music. They were clearly comfortable in each other's company. Every so often Arabella would laugh at something Robert said.

"They make such a handsome couple don't they?" Lady Tremaine said, ostensibly to Arabella's mother, but Emma knew the remark was addressed to her.

She didn't know what to think. When Robert was near, she felt a strange excitement she had not known before, and when he had kissed her, she had felt her insides turn to water. He had held her until she had almost felt part of him, and then he had coldly dismissed her. How could something that had moved her so much have left him so unmoved?

In her heart, Emma knew Lady Tremaine was right. Robert and Arabella were made for each other. Their marriage would be a celebrated alliance.

Arabella played and sang prettily. There was no doubt that she had a pure voice. She even persuaded Robert to join her in a duet or two, his rich baritone providing a contrast to her soprano.

Presently Arabella declared she must rest and turned to Emma. "Come, Miss Smith, perhaps you could play something for us."

"I'm not sure if I can," Emma stammered.

"Why don't you try, Emma," Robert said quietly. "It might prompt you to remember and if it does not, it does not matter. You will have lost nothing. Come, I'll sit with you."

Arabella returned to her seat with the other ladies who began to compliment her on her playing and singing, making it obvious they were not interested in whether Emma could play or not.

"You seem very tense," Robert observed as she sat beside him.

"Why does this surprise you, Your Grace, when I am about to follow the most accomplished young lady of her season and I don't even know if I can actually play this thing?" she hissed.

He grinned. One thing Emma was not short of was spirit. "Just try. See? They're not even listening," he said smoothly, though he was aware of their snub and not pleased by it.

Emma glared at him and placed her fingers on the keys. Then a strange thing happened. Her whole body relaxed as she ran her fingers up and down a scale. From somewhere deep inside, she remembered. Her fingers flew across the keys as notes rose and fell. She played pieces by Mozart, Bach, and Handel. While she was playing, her fears about her memory fell away and she was absorbed in the music.

Finally, she stopped, aware of a silence in the room. The ladies had stopped talking and were looking at her almost with their mouths open. The Earl did have his mouth open and Robert had a wide smile on his face. There was a spontaneous round of applause.

"Splendid, most splendid." The Earl smiled widely. "If ladies could perform in public, you could earn your living at it."

"You are too kind, my Lord," Emma returned his smile.

"Well, my dear, you certainly seem to be able to surprise us," Lady Tremaine added. Emma felt she had passed some kind of test.

The Earl demanded his wife and daughter make up a table of cards, leaving Emma sitting alone on the sofa. Robert joined her.

"Are you sure you should be sitting so close?" Emma asked.

He frowned. "We're not in the gossip salons in London, Emma. Besides, I want to know whether discovering you can play the pianoforte brought back further memories."

"My mother taught me to play I think, I have a memory of a woman in a lavender dress sitting with me at her knee playing. When I was older, she would sit beside me and I would play for her. I have another memory of me playing alone in a large room. I think… I think my mother must be dead because when I was playing I had the feeling that she loved me. If she was alive, she would have come looking for me, wouldn't she?" Emma turned to him, her eyes huge with unshed tears.

He wanted to pull her into his arms and comfort her, to wipe away her tears and enfold her in his embrace, but he could not. Even in the more relaxed atmosphere of Hampshire such behaviour was not acceptable. He had to be content with patting her arm.

"I'm sure your mother loved you, Emma. How could she not? As to whether she is alive and why no one has come looking for you, of course we don't know what direction you came from and the snow has made travelling difficult. After Christmas, we will place an advertisement in *The Times*. Try not to let it worry you. You are getting better and your memory is beginning to return."

"Come, Robert," Arabella trilled, "you simply must tell me about the preparations for the ball. I am dying to know." The card game was over and when Robert looked at where Emma had been, her place was empty.

"I believe Miss Smith has gone to bed," Countess Walmesly informed him. "She said not to bother you."

* * * *

In her room, Emma reviewed the events of the evening. She was more confused than ever. Although it appeared Robert was about to offer for Lady Arabella, his heart wasn't in it. Surely a man who was on the brink of a proposal would not be kissing another woman. Robert was an

36

honourable man, and there was something more, he acted as though he really cared about her. She cared for him, she cared too much. Lying in bed, her thoughts turned to the events of the evening and the memories that had returned. She was relieved she was beginning to remember her life, but something made her uneasy. She had a feeling not all her memories would be good ones.

Chapter Seven

The following morning, the house was in turmoil as the preparations for the Solstice Ball began in earnest. Garlands of holly and ivy were being wound around the grand staircase. Every servant had been pressed into service. There was much to do and only two days remained before the ball. Emma was arranging evergreens on the mantelpiece in the grand salon when Arabella entered.

"Where's Whitney?" she demanded. "That fool of a housekeeper says I must share a maid and the girl she has sent has absolutely no idea of fashion's needs."

"With so much to do for the Ball, all the servants are very busy," Emma replied, fixing the last garland in place.

"It is simply not to be borne. I shall tell Whitney I will not be dictated to by his housekeeper. She will be lucky to retain her position. Why are you doing that?" she snapped. "A lady would leave it for the servants."

"What's the problem, Bella? Because my money would be on Mrs. Frazer every time," a male voice said.

"James? When did you arrive?" Arabella beamed, the scowl replaced by a broad smile.

"A few moments ago. And who is this? Please introduce me." A more boyish version of Robert stood before Emma, grinning widely.

"This young lady is staying here," Arabella replied. "She had a head injury and can no longer remember who she is. Currently she is called Smith. Miss Emma Smith, this is Lord James Tremaine."

"Delighted to make your acquaintance, Miss Smith." He bowed and kissed Emma's hand. "The circumstances are somewhat unfortunate for you, but I consider myself fortunate to meet you. I shall make it my duty to help you to remember who you are."

Emma could not help but laugh at his outrageous attitude. "I am very pleased to make your acquaintance, Lord Tremaine."

"Please call me James, or if that is not enough to pacify the easily scandalised society matrons, Lord James." He grinned again before turning back to Arabella. "Now Bella, what's the problem with Mrs. Frazer?"

"Oh nothing, just a small misunderstanding. Come, I'll take you to your mother. I believe Whitney is meeting with his estate staff." She swept from the room.

"I look forward to seeing you at luncheon, Miss Smith."

* * * *

The two brothers were obviously close Emma noted as she sat in the window seat. They had spent the day outdoing each other with stories of their youth and good-naturedly poking fun at each other. James' lively personality brought out a lighter side in Robert. Even Lady Arabella responded well to James' teasing.

The house was ready for the Solstice Ball. The evergreen garlands had been tied with red ribbons and silver bells which glittered in the candle light. Robert had brought a large tree into the hall and it too was decorated with bells and candles. He had seen something like it on his travels in Austria. It looked beautiful.

Emma thought she would never be able to forget the scent of pine. She was certain she had never seen such a thing before and probably never would again. Once Christmas was over, she would leave Charleton Court. She could not remain indefinitely and could probably find some sort of employment as a companion or pianoforte teacher. Lady Tremaine might even be able to help her find something. She smiled to herself. Lady Tremaine would be so glad to get rid of her, she would probably provide her with a reference herself.

Emma glanced to where Robert and Arabella were seated on the sofa, her fair hair contrasting with his dark head. They were leafing through Arabella's sketch book and she frequently turned to him as he commented on something he had seen.

"They make a fine couple don't they?" Lord James sat down, following her line of vision.

"I believe an announcement is due any day," Emma responded.

"So my mother and Bella's father would hope," James replied enigmatically.

"You don't think his Grace will offer?" Emma could not stop herself from asking.

"Oh, Bella has all the qualities that would make her a marvellous Duchess. There is just one thing my mother has overlooked. Robert has known her since she was born, and they just do not suit. Marriage for them would be a disaster. Within two years they would be living separate and unhappy lives tied to each other for life. Neither of them deserves that."

Emma looked at James, curiously. "I understand many marriages among the ton are like that."

"Yes, and look how unhappy most of them are. Once the inheritance is secure, husbands and wives go their separate ways. It is not what I would want from a marriage nor, I think, my brother either What about you, Miss Smith?" He turned the full force of his gaze on her.

"I doubt that I shall marry at all, Lord Tremaine."

"Why so?"

She took a deep breath. "Well, in the first place, I cannot marry until I know who I am. In the second place, as no one, family or husband, has appeared searching for me, I believe myself to be an orphan. So it follows that I must make my own way in the world."

"Life is not particularly kind to women who have little money and no male to protect them," he observed.

"Life is not particularly kind to anyone with little money," she shot back. "A single woman has a degree of choice denied to a married one. A married woman merely changes from obeying her father to obeying her husband."

Lord James quirked an eyebrow. "What very modern ideas you have, Miss Smith, and yet look at Bella, do you seriously think she will want the freedom that being a spinster will bring?"

Emma looked over at Arabella. "I believe Lady Arabella will probably obey her husband as well as she obeys her father," she conceded.

"That does not bode well for my brother." Lord James laughed. "Though I imagine most women would obey any man for the chance to be addressed as 'Your Grace.'"

Emma shook her head. "What a low opinion of women you have, my lord. You men have so many ways of making your mark on the world while women have so few opportunities. Largely they are lauded for being the wives and mothers of great men."

Lord James looked at her thoughtfully. "You have a most interesting outlook on life, Miss Smith. I wonder if Robert is aware of the forward thinker he has brought into his home."

Lady Arabella closed her sketchbook, bringing their *tete-a-tete* to an abrupt end. Robert was staring into the fire.

"James, what are you and Miss Smith whispering about?"

"Miss Smith was enlightening me with her rather modern ideas about wives and daughters."

Lady Arabella looked at Robert. "A woman's duty is to marry and have children. As a wife, she should be decorative and do everything she can to enhance her husband's life."

Amused, Robert turned and looked at Emma. "And how do your views differ, Miss Smith?"

Emma returned his look. "I believe women need to have control of their own money and, perhaps with better education, they could contribute more to public life."

The Earl laughed. "Really Miss Smith, Arabella cannot keep account of her pin money. I always have to give her more at the end of the month. Heaven knows what a mess she would get in if she had control of her dowry."

"But that's my point," Emma continued. "If girls had a better education, they would be better prepared to take responsibility for themselves."

Lady Arabella wrinkled her nose. "I always hated mathematics and all those hateful fractions and angles."

"That's true," her father agreed. "Her governesses used to despair."

"With respect, Sir," James said, laughing. "I remember Bella as a girl and there were several reasons why her governesses despaired of her."

"If Miss Smith voiced these opinions, I imagine her governesses also

41

despaired," Robert added drily.

"Oh come, brother," James interjected. "Don't tell me you want some ignorant, meek and mild wife. You'd be bored within the first year."

"Thank you, brother. I shall be sure to take your advice."

"I should be most interested to know where these outlandish ideas came from," Lady Tremaine announced. "For if you are to find a husband with some degree of fortune, I imagine you may struggle to find one who agrees with you."

Emma thought for a moment, slowly, pieces and thoughts were coming together in her mind. There were still large gaps, but she was beginning to feel her memory was not lost forever.

"I believe I learned this from a tutor," she replied.

"Well, I for one think this conversation has gone on for long enough, Miss Smith. You will have to learn the real world is the domain of men. It has been so for hundreds of years and will continue to be so for many more. It will not change to accommodate you," Lady Tremaine said. "Now we have all had a long day. I think it is time we retired."

Later, when he sat alone in the library, Robert contemplated the events of the evening. Emma never ceased to surprise him. He had never really thought about what a woman might want out of a marriage. He had thought, like all men, that a wife would be satisfied with her life at home, children, perhaps doing some charitable works. He had assumed because all the women he had known seemed to be happy with their gowns, needlework, music, and art that that was what they were happy and content to do. Emma's ideas intrigued him.

He knew he didn't want marriage to a meek, biddable, obedient wife who would bore him within a month nor did he want a ton marriage of convenience where the only bond between them would be the heirs he sired. He wanted a partner, someone who would work with him, would challenge, and excite him, in bed and out of it. He paused, his brandy glass halfway to his lips. There was only one woman whose name came to his mind.

Chapter Eight

Emma sat with a book on her lap, but mostly looked out at the white, frozen landscape when James and Arabella entered the room.

"Come, Miss Smith, wrap up," James said. "The lake is perfect for skating,"

"Skating?"

"Ice skating, we have lots of skates so I'm sure there will be some to fit." James was taking the book from her hands and setting it down on the window seat as he spoke.

"Perhaps Miss Smith does not skate?" Arabella suggested.

"Then I'll teach her," said a familiar deep voice from the doorway.

Emma's heart thudded as she took in the sight of Robert, his long legs encased in tight buckskin trousers, disappearing into fine black boots. His jacket emphasised the width of his shoulders. He was already shrugging on a top coat.

"I'm not sure…" Emma began.

"Then now is a good time to find out. James and Arabella, you go ahead. I'll wait for Miss Smith," Robert announced.

Within minutes, Emma was dressed in a dark emerald skating costume trimmed with white fur. There was even a matching muff and hat. "Is there no limit to the clothes the duke's sister had?" she said to Alice as she picked up the skates.

"Her ladyship was very fashionable. Most of the clothes are from when she had her season. Young men used to write poems about her."

"Poems?"

"Lot of nonsense if you ask me," Alice sniffed. "Young men with nothing better to do, but," she added, "Lady Sophie is a real lady, kind as well as beautiful, not like some." Alice immediately looked horrified and clapped her hand over her mouth. "I'm sorry Miss, I shouldn't have spoken out of turn like that. My mum says my tongue will get me into trouble."

Emma laughed. "Don't worry, Alice, I imagine, my mother may have said the same."

A sharp stab of pain hit her in her chest. Would she ever remember her mother? She felt like a little boat adrift at sea, not knowing where it had come from or where it was going. Giving herself a brisk mental shake, Emma headed for the door. If she kept busy and active, that black, hollow feeling was kept at bay.

"Wish me luck, Alice. I'm not sure whether I will come back in one piece or several."

Robert was waiting in the hall, idly tapping his gloves against his leg as she made her way down the stairs. His breath caught in his throat. The green costume emphasised her shapely figure and creamy skin. Her hair was neatly coiled under the jaunty hat, but as usual one or two tendrils had escaped, making his fingers itch to tuck them in place.

"You look like a snow princess," he said, taking the skates and slinging them over his shoulder with his own, before offering his arm.

"Thank you. I only hope I don't look like a snowman at the end of this." She smiled and could not help being pleased by his compliment.

"Oh," Emma said as she looked in wonderment at the fairytale scene before her. Snow laden trees overhung the edges of the lake. The sun made the ice sparkle and the snow looked like icing. In the middle of the lake, the bird house looked like a miniature ice palace. James and Arabella were already on the lake, laughing as they gracefully glided past, forwards and backwards, separately and together.

"I'm not sure about this, Your Grace," Emma whispered as Robert adjusted her skates. 'I don't think I have done this before.'

"That's what you said about the pianoforte," he said, smiling. "Look what happened there."

He stood up and held out his hand. "Come on, you will enjoy it."

An hour later, Emma laughed. "Well, Sir, I was beginning to think you lied most cruelly about the enjoyment part, but I think I am now able to skate without flailing like a beached whale for all of ten yards."

Robert laughed as he glided past her backwards. "You're doing very well. You just need a little more confidence and some speed." He spun and came towards her. "You need to take longer strides." Without warning, one arm was around her waist and the other hand captured hers and she was pulled close as he skated smoothly forwards.

Emma tried to match her strides to his. The only sound was their skates as they scraped across the surface of the ice.

"I suggest you try to breathe at the same time, Miss Smith. Relax, feel the rhythm."

Robert's lips were so close to her ear she could feel his breath. She found it even more disturbing than careering around a frozen lake on thin pieces of metal.

"Forgive me, Sir, but I find it difficult to relax at this speed." To say nothing of being held tightly to his side.

"Nonsense, you no doubt go at much greater speed on that horse of yours."

"That's different. When I'm on Apollo, I am in control."

"Well then, time to take control." As quickly as he had held her waist, he let go, turned, and skated backwards just out of reach in front of her.

They were well away from the safety of the edge. "You wretch," she cried. "You let me go."

He held out his hands. "All you have to do is reach for me. I'm right here. Just keep up the long strides you were doing. Don't look down, Emma. Look at me." His voice was soft and coaxing.

She did as she was bid, and they travelled almost the length of the lake with Robert just out of reach. With each stride she gained confidence until her blade edge caught on a rut in the ice at the very moment Robert looked to where James and Arabella were performing a pirouette. In an instant, Robert was on his back and she was lying on his chest. Emma was mortified.

"Sir, Your Grace. Robert, are you all right?" Robert's eyes were closed. She touched his face. "Oh my good Lord, I've just killed a duke, a peer of the realm," she whispered, struggling to get up before an arm came around and held her still.

"This," said an amused voice, "has been the most fun I have had ice skating since Hunter decided to serve tea to my mother on his skates, and were it not for the fact that my nether regions are freezing, I would be happy to continue in my role as your mattress."

Truth to tell, however cold it was, one part of his nether regions felt no cold at all. Robert knew that were it not for the fact James and Arabella were with them, he could not and would not have resisted the temptation to kiss Emma. The experience of her lying on top of him was enough to arouse a man made of stone, and he most certainly was not

By the time James and Arabella noticed them, Robert was already on his feet and dusting himself down.

"Do my eyes deceive me?" James teased. "Did you actually take a fall, brother?"

"I most certainly did not. Miss Smith took a fall, and I merely laid myself gallantly beneath her to act as her cushion." Robert grinned.

"Then how about a race, brother?" James challenged.

"Are you sure you want the humiliation, brother?"

"I have the advantage of youth on my side," the younger man retorted.

"Maturity and experience will always beat the callowness of youth," Robert replied loftily.

"They have always been like this," Arabella explained. "From small children they have always competed from bowling hoops to target shooting and everything in between."

"And one day I intend to win." James laughed.

The two brothers skated effortlessly to the start line whilst Emma and Arabella settled themselves on a fallen log. Once alone with Arabella, Emma felt uncomfortable. She was sitting with the woman who was going to marry the man she loved.

Keeping her voice neutral she spoke. "Who do you think will win your ladyship?"

Arabella's gaze followed the passage of the two men. "Oh Whitney, unless he chooses to allow James to win which I very much doubt. Whitney is used to getting what he wants." She turned to Emma. "As am I."

"I don't doubt it," Emma replied.

"Miss Smith, you really need to understand that your flirtation with Whitney means nothing to him. If anything, he is mildly amused by your gaucheness, but do not imagine it will go any further. Were it not for his rescue of you, making him feel he has some responsibility, you would have been sent on your way. Someone like you is not usually received at Charlton." Arabella's tone dripped contempt.

Were it not for the fact that the brothers were about to race, Emma would have walked away. However, she would not give Arabella the satisfaction of knowing how her words had hurt. It was true there was no point in hoping there could ever be anything between her and Robert. She was a mild diversion until she left and nothing more. Relationships between handsome princes or dukes were for fairytales. Things like that never happened in the real world.

"Thank you for clarifying the situation, Lady Walmesly. I am obliged for your candour and the generosity of spirit you showed in setting matters straight. Now, while I am still a guest of his grace the duke, perhaps we should watch the race.'

As predicted, Robert won.

"But it was close." James protested, good naturedly as the four walked back to the house.

"You are very quiet, Miss Smith," Robert observed. "Are you tired?"

Emma painted on a bright smile. "Not a bit, Your Grace. Lady Walmesly and I were having a discussion about social conventions and values and her ladyship has given me much to think about."

Robert looked speculatively at Arabella's back as she said something that made James laugh. He could not imagine Arabella having a serious discussion about anything other than the price of bonnets and gowns. He frowned, the sparkle in Emma's eyes and the glow in her cheeks had gone.

Chapter Nine

Although a slight thaw had taken place, there was still a great deal of snow, but the turnpikes were largely passable. The house was alive with the sounds of guests arriving for the ball. Many were staying for a day or so.

Lady Tremaine mellowed as many of her friends arrived. "It's so good to see the house full of life again," she observed.

Emma had made herself as useful as she could. Even Lady Tremaine had relied on her to help settling her friends.

Eventually there had been a lull and Emma had escaped to the stables. She was feeding a carrot to Apollo when Robert found her.

"Are you hiding, Miss Smith?" he asked, leaning casually against the wall.

She ran her hand along the horse's neck. "Of course not, well perhaps a little," she conceded. He quirked an eyebrow. "I just feel so stupid," she explained, carefully addressing her remarks to the horse. "People want to know who I am and I cannot tell them, so they look at me with pity and then embarrassment. They do not know what to do and neither do I. Some of them clearly think I am here under false pretenses."

He stepped forward, put his hands on her arms, and pulled her around to face him. When she continued to look down, he put a finger under her chin and tipped her face up to his.

"Miss Smith, it does not matter what these people think. You are a beautiful young woman who is brave and clever. When they have been in your company for a minute, anyone with any intelligence at all would realise that. As for the snobbish ones, half of them have no brains and the others are only in privileged positions because one of their ancestors held a towel while some king or other wiped his ar... hands. It is a good thing they inherited some money because some of them have neither the brains nor sense to make any for themselves."

In spite of her concerns, Emma could not help but laugh. "If you were trying to make me feel better, Your Grace, you have succeeded."

He smiled down at her. "Good, I like to hear you laugh. Now that I have made you feel better, I think it only fair that you should do the same for me."

"And how can I do that, Sir?" Emma's mouth suddenly felt dry.

"I want you to say my name. It's Robert." His voice was seductively low.

"I know what it is, Your Grace. I just don't think—"

"No, Emma, don't think, just say it. I want to hear my name on your lips."

They were standing so close Emma could feel the heat from his hands spread through her body. She could barely breathe. The air around them had become thick.

"It's an easy name, only two syllables," he continued. He was now so close she felt sure he would hear the beating of her heart.

"Very well... Robert," she whispered.

"It's not enough," he muttered as he drew her into his arms. "Now I want to feel your lips on mine."

His lips grazed hers, then his tongue teased her lips open, deepening the kiss and molding her body to his, her soft curves to the hard planes of his. He wanted to hear Emma call his name over and over when he took her to the peak of passion he instinctively knew their lovemaking would bring.

Her arms snaked around his neck and soft sighs and whimpers came from her throat unbidden. He intended that she would never forget this moment. She would be forever branded by the feel of his lips on hers.

Suddenly, Robert drew back. He had done it again. She was a young, vulnerable woman, and he had yet again compromised her. He frankly conceded, if he had gone on much longer, he would have thrown her in the straw and taken her there. He had never wanted a woman as he wanted her. He had always been in total control where women were concerned, and he did not like the fact that with Miss Emma Smith he seemed to have no control whatsoever.

His reason reasserted itself now that there was some distance between them. His face hardened into harsh lines. "I apologise, Miss Smith. That should not have happened. I shall leave now and suggest you wait for a few moments before you follow. I will ensure you are appropriately chaperoned henceforth." He turned and strode away, before he gave in to the temptation to tuck the stray strand of hair behind her ear. He must not touch her again.

Emma watched him leave with mounting anger. What sort of man would kiss her as though his life depended on it and then leave? Twice. He had said he was no gentleman and she was beginning to believe it. She turned back to Apollo, running her fingers along the soft velvet of his nose soothing both her and him.

"Ah, Miss Smith, I am about to take a turn around the Long Gallery, would you care to accompany me?" Lady Arabella stood at the doorway. "There is something I need to discuss with you."

"Of course," Emma replied, knowing that it was not so much an invitation as a command.

They walked in silence until it was broken by Arabella. "Miss Smith, I do not intend to beat about the bush. You need to leave as soon as possible. Your presence here is something of an embarrassment. The duke and I are practically betrothed, and Whitney, as a man of honour does not feel he can ask you to leave. Believe me, Miss Smith, no one wants you here."

"Believe me, my lady, I am equally anxious to leave," Emma replied.

"As to your outrageous outburst the other evening, well we are all hoping you will hold your tongue this evening and do nothing to further embarrass your host."

Emma could feel her temper beginning to rise. "Let me assure you, my lady, I have no intention of embarrassing myself or anyone else, though I should consider ignorance and stupidity to be a greater source of embarrassment than the ability to discuss a matter with logical argument. Now if you will excuse me, I believe I shall go and dress for the ball." Emma turned and strode from the gallery, glad to leave the passive eyes of proud generations of Tremaines and the angry eyes of one who, according to her own account, would soon be one of them.

Still fuming, Emma marched to her room. If what Arabella said was true, Robert was not just toying with her emotions but those of Arabella as well. Perhaps she should have told Arabella what had happened a few moments before she had entered the stables. Well, if they were to marry, good luck to them. They deserved each other.

She stopped short when she saw the dress Alice was laying out on the bed. "Alice, where did that come from?"

Alice beamed. "Isn't it lovely, Miss? His Grace ordered it from Madame Deshayes. He said his sister's hand-me-downs were not suitable for you to wear at the ball. Madame Deshayes's girls have worked night and day to get it ready for you."

It was gorgeous. The bodice was of the most striking blue she had seen, shot through with silver thread. The overskirt was of fine silver gauze sprinkled with tiny seed pearls that gleamed as they caught the light. There were matching kid slippers.

"As you say, Alice, it's lovely, but I can't accept it. Please put it away, and I'll wear the rose muslin.'

Alice's face fell. "His Grace was most insistent, Miss. He said I was not to take no for an answer and that he would see you in the library to explain. He had Mrs. Frazer remove all your other dresses." She opened the wardrobe door.

Emma could not believe her eyes. "Of all the high handed, impossible, autocratic.... Well, we'll see about this."

Robert was sitting at his desk, his estate manager opposite him when Emma marched into the room. "Would you excuse us for a moment, Hughes?"

The bewildered estate manager looked from one to the other. Emma's thunderous expression was met by Robert's mild amusement. Another look at Emma and the manager began gathering his papers.

"Very good, Your Grace. If I may make so bold, I shall work on the papers in another room until Your Grace is free again. We can discuss the other matter later."

Robert waited until the door closed before turning his attention to Emma. The two spots of colour on her cheeks were a clear indication that she was angry. "Now, Miss Smith, you wanted to see me?" he began mildly.

"Frankly, Your Grace, I doubt that I shall ever want to see you again, but that is beside the point. I cannot accept the ball gown. It is too much along with the fact that a single man should not buy dresses for a single woman. People will think the very worst. They will think that I am your…"

"Mistress?" Robert provided helpfully. Truth to tell he had briefly thought of that himself when he had ordered the dress, but he didn't want Emma as his mistress He wanted much more than a willing bed partner—he wanted her, body and soul.

"Exactly so," Emma continued. "You are the most impossible man. You keep telling me you will not compromise my honour and then you kiss me, and now this dress. It is too much, Your Grace. I do not know who I am. I do not know my past, but in order to make a future for myself, I have to have a spotless reputation, otherwise no family will employ me."

Try as she might, she could not stop the single tear as it followed a path down her cheek. She turned to go, desperate for the duke not to see her in tears. Her pride did not want him to see her give in to the fear that had stalked her since she had woken from her fall.

She had taken only three steps before Robert blocked her path. For a powerful man, he moved with speed and grace. He pulled her into his arms, folding her close to offer his body for comfort.

Emma was undone. Burying her face in his chest, she wept. All the while Robert spoke softly to her, trying to soothe her as great sobs wracked her body.

She had been so brave, coping without complaint, trying to make herself useful, and artlessly making him fall in love with her. He paused at that. For the first time in his life, he was in love. He smiled to himself. He had always dismissed the idea of love.

Men married for heirs and women for security and status, but now he saw he would never be happy or satisfied with anything less. The smile turned to a frown. He could not propose to Emma now. Firstly, he had to deal with the issue of Arabella. Much as he knew their marriage would be a disaster, he had to extricate himself from the situation without damaging Arabella's prospects, not that he had ever encouraged her to think there would be a match. He knew both their mothers had encouraged her to believe it. He experienced a pang of guilt. He should have scotched the idea long ago. Secondly, he could not marry Emma while she still did not know who she was. It would not be fair to her. He would have to be patient and wait for her to recover and he could find her family. He sighed, he had never been that patient.

Emma raised her tear stained face, "I apologise Your Grace."

Robert put a long finger on her lips. "You do not need to apologise, Miss Smith. Let me explain a little. I ordered the dress because although Sophie's gowns have been made to fit you well, Alice told me there was no ball gown among them. I did not want you to feel at a disadvantage among the other women at the ball." He smiled. "I also knew you would refuse to wear it, hence the clearing of the wardrobe."

"Thank you for your kindness, Your Grace," Emma murmured. "I don't believe I have ever seen a more beautiful dress."

"Then indulge me, wear it and enjoy the ball, and afterwards we will talk about the future, I promise."

Emma managed a watery smile. "Thank you, Your Grace."

Might as well be hung for a sheep as a lamb. He reached behind to the drawer of his desk. "I would like you to wear these to go with the dress." He held out a box. "Open it."

Emma looked as though he was handing her a snake. She firmly put her hands behind her back. "I would rather not."

"You don't even know what's in the box," he teased.

She raised her eyes to his. "I may be naïve, but even I recognise a jewellery box."

"Most women like opening jewel boxes." His eyes met hers.

"I am not most women," she shot back.

"I am beginning to understand that." He sighed, opening the box himself.

Emma could not help a gasp as she took in the fabulous suite of diamonds and pearls.

"These are the Whitney diamonds. I want you to wear them tonight. The gown was designed for them."

She raised her eyes to his. He almost laughed out loud at her horrified expression.

"Your Grace, I cannot possibly wear these jewels. They are priceless. What if they got lost or broken, or—"

"Like the gown, Emma, I wanted you to feel confident at the ball. The other women will be wearing jewels. I don't want you to feel at a disadvantage."

"But it's too much."

"Emma, wear the jewels. I would like to see them do justice to the gown." He spoke quietly, thinking he would like to see her just wearing the jewels.

"Is that a command, Your Grace?"

"It is a request and less of the 'Your Grace' please. You make me feel like an old man with gout."

"Then I shall be sure to wave as I dance past you in your armchair by the fire," Emma teased.

A frown wrinkled Robert's handsome features at the thought of Emma dancing with another man. "Impertinent Miss, I insist on two dances."

Reluctantly he let Emma go. The room always seemed to have a little less life when she left it. He idly contemplated the fire.

A discreet cough sounded as Hughes entered the room. "If it please, Your Grace, I believe may have some information regarding the young lady. A man has been enquiring about a missing young person in the village yesterday, Your Grace."

"Do you know who this man was?"

"Not yet, Your Grace."

"Find him. Tonight."

Chapter Ten

Emma peeped over the banister before she began her entrance to the ball. The house could not have looked more festive. The scents of clove and cinnamon mingled with the pine from the tree. The chandeliers were ablaze with light and reflected in the brilliance of the diamonds, emeralds, and rubies adorning the throats and wrists of the women. Lady Tremaine looked regal and resplendent in a peacock blue gown while Arabella's beauty was shown off to perfection in a fine, white gauze shot through with gold. At her throat and ears were the Walmesly sapphires. She stood with her mother surrounded by a group of young men each eagerly vying for her attention which she bestowed with indifference.

Alice gave Emma the tiniest nudge. "Go on, Miss."

Emma turned. Alice had quickly become an ally. "Wish me luck."

"You don't need luck, Miss." Her maid grinned. "All those young men will be wanting to marry you by the end of the evening."

Emma grimaced and began her descent.

Robert had been standing talking to his brother and became aware James was no longer listening to him. He turned, and for a second, he could have sworn his heart had stopped. The room gradually fell silent as Emma made her way down the staircase. By now, all the guests had heard of the mysterious girl who had lost her memory and they were all keen to get a glimpse of her. Her smile wobbled as she became aware of the scrutiny.

He stepped forward. "Ladies and gentlemen, many of you have no doubt heard that Miss Smith is residing under my roof at the moment while she recovers from her accident. I shall be happy to introduce you to her presently, but in the meanwhile I believe we should begin the festivities."

He offered Emma his arm and they led the way through to the ballroom where the musicians began with a minuet. "By the way," Robert whispered as they joined hands, "you look ravishing tonight."

He was seriously thinking he should have had the dressmaker produce something in sackcloth. He had seen the looks on the faces of the other men in the room, including his brother and, he had to admit to himself, he didn't like it. She was like an ethereal goddess, making the other women look garish in comparison.

"I should, however, appreciate it if you could look as though you are vaguely enjoying the experience," he added wryly. "Try to breathe. I find it helps enormously, regardless of the task I am undertaking. I was right, by the way, about the jewels."

Emma looked up, nervously touching the diamonds that blazed around her slender throat, and he was rewarded with a smile. "I'm sorry, Your Grace. I am trying not to lose any diamonds and not to injure you. I fear I now remember that I seem to have two left feet."

Robert laughed. "I have survived the battlefields of Europe, Miss Smith. I believe I will survive the onslaught of your small feet."

Although Robert wanted to dance every dance with Emma, his duties as host meant he had to circulate. He noticed with more than a little irritation, that Emma was not short of partners. Every time he sought her on the dance floor, she seemed to be whirling past him with yet another young buck who had sought an introduction from either his mother or his brother. Either way, he felt that one, or both of them were trying to sabotage his plan, which his mother most certainly would have, had she known about it.

"She is most beguiling." He had not noticed his brother join him as he lounged against a marble pillar at the edge of the floor.

"Indeed," he agreed.

"Why the frown, brother? Is it because Lord Yately is perhaps holding Miss Smith a little too close for your comfort?" Amusement coloured James' voice.

"Yately is a rake, and Miss Smith is too innocent to realise what she is dealing with there," Robert responded grimly.

"I don't know." James continued, helping himself to a glass of champagne as a servant passed. "She seems to be doing quite well. When he tries to get too close, Miss Smith steps on his foot."

"I think she needs to tread on another part of his anatomy for him to get the message."

James chuckled. "Well, well, well, I believe the Duke of Whitney is smitten."

"Don't be ridiculous," Robert snapped. "I am merely concerned for a young lady who currently is under my protection as a guest in this house."

"That being so, if you don't mind, brother, I think I shall ask Arabella for the waltz."

"Why should I mind?"

"Why indeed?" James replied cryptically before sauntering off in Arabella's direction.

Robert was about to ensure he was on Emma's card for the waltz when Hunter appeared at his side. "A gentleman has arrived, Your Grace, who says he is here regarding Miss Smith. I've put him in the library, Sir. He seems most insistent that he see you now."

The man was standing by the fire when Robert entered the library. He was a good head and shoulders shorter than Robert's imposing six feet. He still wore his greatcoat but a beaver hat lay on the sofa, along with a riding crop and gloves. Robert could see from his clothes that he was a gentleman, but when he turned, his once handsome face had clearly paid the price for many years of drinking—his complexion was ruddy and his features coarse.

The man gave a small bow. "I'm sorry to disturb, Your Grace, but I believe you have my niece."

"And you are?" Robert's voice was as icy as his eyes.

"Sir Clifford Hammond. We are staying at Ellerton Grange, the property my sister inherited from her grandmother. Poor Eleanor was never able to visit it before she died. It will be part of Emmy's dowry now I suppose. Emmy's mother was my sister. I took them in when William died. I raised that girl as if she was my own daughter. I am grateful for you for looking after Emmy, but if you would fetch her, we will be on our way."

"I'm afraid that won't be possible," Robert said firmly. "Miss Smith had a head injury and has lost her memory. It is returning slowly, but she is in no fit state to travel especially at this time of night and in this weather."

"Miss Smith? Her name is Emily, Emily Francesca Conrad, though we have called her Emmy since she was a baby."

Robert's mind went back to the moment when they had decided on the name Emma. She had felt something stir in her memory and the two names were not dissimilar.

"Emmy is quite a horsewoman," the older man continued. "I am sure I can bring her to her senses sharpish."

Robert glanced at the riding crop. His temper rose. So this was the man who had beaten Emma… Emily so brutally. He took a breath to regain control.

"Perhaps, Sir Clifford, you might know what led Miss Sm... Conrad to leave her home during a blizzard?"

The other man flushed. "Emmy is a headstrong young woman. She and I had quarrelled over some trivial thing and she took off."

"Forgive me, Sir Clifford, but when I found Miss Conrad, she had nothing with her, just a thin cloak. Had we not found her when we did, I doubt she would have survived the night. I put it to you that what you argued about cannot have been trivial." His quiet voice masked the fury he felt.

Sir Clifford was not to be intimidated. "It was a family matter, Sir, and none of your concern. Now fetch my niece," he blustered. "Then we'll be on our way."

"Family matter or no, Sir," Robert drawled, "explain to me why Miss Conrad had whip marks about her person."

The older man's face went from red to purple. "What I do to discipline my niece is no concern of yours. A man is entitled to discipline his horse, his dog, his wife, and his child as he sees fit. Emmy is under my care until she marries or until she is five and twenty, when according to her father's will she will inherit her fortune. As she is three and twenty, and I am her guardian and provider, I shall discipline her as I deem necessary. Now get your servant to fetch her or I shall be inclined to drag her out of your ball myself."

Robert glared at Emma's guardian with distaste. He had met men from all walks of life in his career in the army, but none that disgusted him as much as the man in front of him now.

Sir Clifford, sensing victory began to relax. His glance strayed to the decanter on the table. Although good manners dictated that Robert should offer his guest some refreshment, he was damned if he was going to offer hospitality to this brute.

"You wanted to see me, Your Grace, though I am most upset that you did not honour our waltz... Oh." Emma had entered the room unannounced.

Her ready smile froze as she saw the man standing a few feet away from her. The colour drained from her cheeks as she stared with horror at her guardian. Like a kaleidoscope, all the fragmented memories that had been whirling and floating without connection suddenly came into focus. The fog that had descended on her brain cleared and she knew who she was, where she was, and most importantly, she knew why.

Robert stared. Before his eyes he could see her transform from the lovely and lively young woman he had fallen in love with to an empty shell. Her eyes lost their lustre and her face lost all expression, even her voice lost life.

"Good evening, Emmy. You have led me a pretty dance, miss. I have come to take you home. Tell his grace who you are so that he is convinced I am not trying to abduct you"

Emily did not move, but lowered her gaze. "I'm sorry, Uncle." She turned to Robert but could not meet his eyes. "I am Miss Emily Francesca Conrad of Ellerton Grange and this is my uncle, Sir Clifford Hammond, my guardian."

"Running off like that, no one knowing what had happened to you, making a nuisance of yourself, and putting this gentleman to a great deal of trouble. I hope you are ashamed of yourself."

Emily was not fooled by his quiet and reasonable tone. Her uncle was furious with her and it was not all because she had been missing for a few days. It was more likely that she had been found alive. Had she died of exposure or a broken neck from her fall, he, as her only living relative, would have been sole heir to her fortune. Now that he had found her very much alive and well, he would have to revert to the plan from which she had been running when Robert found her. The trouble was, she could not think of a way out of her predicament. She was Sir Clifford's ward. She had no money until she was twenty-five. She had no control of anything.

She would rather die than have the humiliation of Robert knowing the true circumstances under which she lived. She kept her gaze on the floor.

"I am sorry I have caused such trouble. I shall get my things and return with you."

Robert watched as she fled from the room. Something was wrong and he intended to get to the bottom of it. Damn the ball that was in full swing. He had a houseful of guests who were obliviously dancing the night away. He excused himself from Sir Clifford and made his way rapidly through the ballroom, greeting guests as though there was nothing amiss, his mind working overtime on what to do.

He caught James' eye. "Look after Arabella, James. Take my dances with her and please escort her into supper."

"Problem, brother?" James's eyes reflected his concern for his brother.

"Nothing I can't handle. Just hold the fort for me here."

James gaze followed his brother as he strode from the room. Whatever it was, Robert would deal with it, of that he had no doubt, but he had not expected the additional bonus of time with Arabella.

* * * *

Sir Clifford sat down, and, as no-one had offered him any refreshment, helped himself to a large glass of Robert's brandy and with a smile, settled himself to wait for Emily's return. Finally, his plans were coming to fruition.

Chapter Eleven

Emily pulled her riding habit from the chest. It was all she had arrived with and that was how she would depart. She was determined her uncle would not benefit from her stay at Charleton Court in any way, including the ball gown she was wearing. As her fingers struggled with the tiny pearl buttons down the back of her dress she regretted telling Alice to enjoy some time in the servants' hall when she heard the door of her room open.

"Thank goodness, Alice. You must have read my mind. Would you help me out of this gown? I need to change and the buttons are such a fiddle." Deft fingers quickly dispensed with the buttons.

"I have to go away, Alice," Emily said. "I can't explain why, but I wanted to say how grateful I have been for your work. You should definitely be looking for a position as a lady's maid, perhaps Lady Tremaine might…" Her voice stilled as she noticed the very male hands that scooped up the gown as she stepped out of it.

"It is one thing for you to run away, but encouraging my servants to leave is not acceptable." Robert's velvet voice dragged her bewildered mind into focus as his hands began the task of unlacing her stays.

Emily spun around. She clutched the dress to cover her. "Your Grace, what are you doing? Are you determined to ruin me?"

"Far from it, Emily. I am trying to save you." He ached to take her into his arms. In his mind's eye he saw her as a young girl, struggling to come to terms with the loss of both of her parents and the hell he could only imagine she had lived with the brute downstairs.

"You cannot, Sir. No one can. I am beholden to my uncle. He has

61

control of my fortune and therefore control of me." She shrugged.

* * * *

Emily had learned early in her life her uncle would stop at nothing to get what he wanted. She took a deep breath and told Robert that after her mother's funeral, her uncle had summoned her and spelled it out. She would be fed, housed, and educated as he saw fit and would marry a man of his choosing. He quoted the will so she would be in no doubt of what it said. Until she came of age at five and twenty or married, he would, as her only living male relative, be her guardian. Should she wish to marry before that time, he would need to give his approval to ensure she did not fall into the clutches of some fortune hunter.

She later learned he was furious that her fortune was in trust and he could only access sufficient funds to pay for her upbringing. He had been counting on a sizeable amount to offset his debts. From his tailor to his wine merchant, he owed money all over the country. He had disappeared to America for a few years, leaving Emily at boarding school. She then tried to manage the estate with the help of some of the older servants who remembered her father. As her guardian, her uncle was needed to release her money she desperately needed to run the house.

Occasionally, the lawyer released some funds but only enough to keep the estate together and only after much negotiation by Emily. She had learned the estate had to be managed to provide the income her uncle was keeping from her. Sometimes she thought he had died or forgotten her. Then a small trickle of money would be released. She knew she had to hang on for just over a year and could claim her inheritance and live as an independent woman, but Sir Clifford had returned with a plan.

Emily was not in the crumbling manor when he arrived back. She had been away, staying with an old school friend who was preparing for her wedding. The visit had been an extended one. Emily had nothing to hurry home to. Had she known what awaited her when she returned, she would never have returned at all.

Her guardian arrived, instantly dismissed the remaining servants, and brought in some of his own. He had also brought a guest, his friend, Sir Richard Cropton, who, he informed Emily, was to become her husband.

Sir Richard had looked her up and down as though he were assessing a prize horse. Her flesh crawled. She felt as though he could see through her clothing.

"I thought you said she was tolerably handsome," he drawled.

"Handsome enough for you." Sir Clifford laughed. "Since when were you so particular about what a woman looked like? Besides," he added, "you can always close your eyes." The two men sniggered.

Emily's mind reeled. "I don't understand, uncle."

His eyes narrowed. "Don't play the innocent miss with me. I told you many years ago I would choose a suitable husband for you and I have. Sir Richard is a good friend of mine. You will marry him as soon as the banns can be read. We shall close this place up and sell it. You will live at Sir Richard's house in Lancashire or Yorkshire or some such place in the north."

"I will never sell Ellerton," Emily replied.

"You will have no say in the matter, miss. When you marry Sir Richard, your property will become his to dispose of as he wishes. Besides, this should have been mine. Your mother only got it because she poisoned your grandmother's mind against me. The stupid cow never liked me. 'You are a wastrel and a profligate, Clifford, and until you mend your ways, you shall not be trusted with anything of worth until you know the value of it,'" he quoted. "I hope the old bitch rots in hell." He looked around. "Where is the decent brandy in this hole?"

For the next two weeks, Emily was a prisoner in her own home. Wherever she went, one of her uncle's new servants went with her. If she went for a ride, one of the grooms rode a short distance behind. If she walked in the gardens, one of the other men was always close by. A walk into the village was always accompanied 'for her protection.' She saw little of her uncle or Sir Richard except at dinner when they both laughed and joked, rarely addressing her.

"Come on, Cropton, drink up." Her uncle slopped yet more claret into their glasses. "You'll soon be a rich man and so will I." They both laughed.

That Sunday banns were read for the first time.

Coming across Sir Richard on his own in the shabby library one afternoon, Emily decided to try appealing to him. Perhaps once he was away from her uncle, he might be more approachable.

She straightened her dress and patted her hair in place before dropping a curtsey. "I wondered if I might have a word, Sir?"

He put down the book he was leafing through and looked at her. "You might."

"It's just that I do not think I can marry you, Sir. I hardly know you and from the little I have seen I do not think we should suit. Truth to tell, Sir," she added, "I do not think you want to marry me either." She held her breath.

He regarded her for some time before replying. "Well, little Miss, you have at last shown some spirit. I shall enjoy that. As your uncle has given you sufficient information, it is not for me to go against his wishes, but I shall tell you my expectations once we are married. Sit down." His tone was reasonable as he gestured to the space beside him. Emily sat, conscious of his thigh brushing hers through the fine material of her gown.

"When we marry, I will become your lord and master. What is yours will become mine. Your property will become mine to do with as I see fit which I shall enjoy very much. Your body will also become mine to do with as I wish and I shall enjoy that very much." He stroked her arm. "Whether you enjoy it will be entirely your own affair."

He moved with lightning speed and before she knew it she was on his lap. His hands roamed all over her body and his lips were on hers. No matter how she struggled, she could not free herself. For all his apparent softness, Sir Richard was extremely strong.

"Ah, the little cat has claws. Struggle away, my dear, I shall enjoy subduing you all the more." He breathed against her throat, one hand clamped around her arms while the other hand travelled up her thigh.

Emily stopped struggling. If he enjoyed her struggles, perhaps he would stop if she was still.

He laughed. "Willing or not, I will have you. It matters not to me and if you do not please me, I shall discipline you until you do, and," he added, his dark eyes glittering, "I shall enjoy that very much."

Emily was frightened now. She was not a total innocent. She knew something of what happened between a man and his wife, but she knew now that Sir Richard was dangerous. He was not interested in a loving relationship with his wife. He wanted control and domination.

"Open your mouth," he commanded. As his mouth ground down on hers, she did as she was bid. "Perhaps I won't wait for the wedding night, perhaps I'll take my pleasure here and now," he muttered, his hands going to the buttons on his breeches. Emily bit his lip as hard as she could.

In a split second he released her, blood pouring from his lip. Emily was across the room and at the door when he called after her. "You'll pay for that, my lady. Remember that on our wedding night. Your deed will not go unpunished. I shall very much enjoy that," he added softly.

Later, her uncle had come to her room, furious at Sir Richard's account of their earlier encounter. She needed, he said, to understand that she would marry Sir Richard and would obey him, even if he had to beat it into her. She watched with horror as he took off his coat and picked up his riding crop. He left twenty minutes later, breathing heavily. Emily waited until he had gone before the tears began to fall.

That Sunday the banns were read for the second time.

It was a conversation she overheard between her uncle and her bridegroom that convinced Emily she had to escape, no matter how dangerous it might be. The two men had been drinking and the library door was ajar. She had not intended to eavesdrop but heard her name.

"Why don't you just have her declared insane and put in an asylum?" Sir Richard said. "You get power of attorney and then it's all yours."

"I might consider that if I had time, but my creditors are getting persistent. I thought you wanted her. She'll provide those heirs."

"Oh, I want her all right, but it isn't to provide heirs. I don't give a damn what happens after I'm dead. The whole pile can fall down as far as I'm concerned. I just want money for the here and now. Your niece will provide for other needs. The trouble is, Clifford, she has been allowed to run wild. She needs to be disciplined. Fortunately, I have always enjoyed that." He laughed.

"You will look after Emmy though? In other circumstances I would have looked after her."

There was a pause and a clinking of glasses as the two men filled their glasses. "Of course, while she pleases me. Just make certain she understands that."

That night, Emily lay in bed, racking her brains for a way out of the situation. Before, she had merely thought of Sir Richard with distaste. Now she was afraid he wouldn't hesitate to have her locked away once he had his hands on her fortune or worse.

Her opportunity came the next afternoon. She was riding back from the village with the groom once again riding behind her when she heard him call that his horse had gone lame and they needed to go back. She had not hesitated. Once the groom was off his horse, she kicked Apollo and galloped in the opposite direction. She had no real idea of where she was going, but she wanted to put as much distance between her and Ellerton before a search party was organised.

Alternating between galloping and trotting and keeping away from the turnpike roads, she rode for several hours. Then the snow started, fine flakes at first, then large flakes. As it settled, she had difficulty in seeing the contours of the land and Apollo was getting tired. She decided she would stop for the night and try and find shelter. She felt confident she was far enough away from Ellerton to approach one of the farmers and ask if she could shelter in a barn.

A stag darted across her path and Apollo reared. Her numb hands slipped on the reins and she fell to the ground. The next thing she remembered was waking up in the Blue Room.

Chapter Twelve

Robert listened to her story in total silence, his arms folded across his chest. The silence between them stretched as though time had stopped.

Emily bit her lip. "I'm so sorry to have brought this trouble into your house, Your Grace. If you would leave, I will dress and be away from Charleton before your other guests are aware of the disturbance."

That galvanised him. "The hell you will," he growled. "I'll tell you what we are going to do." He hauled her ball gown up and only slightly more slowly than he had unfastened the buttons, he re-did them. "We are going back to speak to your uncle and when we have done that, we are going back to the ball."

Emily was bewildered. "I don't understand."

He turned her to face him, his large hands circling her arms with enough strength to hold her but without exerting any pressure. "Emily, Miss Conrad, the last thing I am about to do is to let you go back to your uncle. All I ask is that you trust me." His eyes blazed into hers.

"I do trust you, Sir, you have given me no reason not to," she responded simply.

"My God, Emily." His arms went around her. He groaned as her lips opened to his, allowing his tongue to explore her mouth. When she tentatively touched his tongue with hers, a bolt of lightning swept through his body. He pulled her closer, wanting her, but he could not, not yet, but soon he promised himself.

Emily felt bereft as he stepped back, his hands dropping to his sides. She could hardly breathe, let alone think, when she was in his arms all she

67

wanted to do was to melt into him. When he kissed her, her entire being seemed to concentrate only on where she was connected to him. She would savour that last kiss between them.

In a few minutes, whatever he said, she would have to leave Charleton forever. Her uncle had the law on his side, so the memory of that kiss would have to last her a life-time. It was not a memory of what might have been. She was too realistic to know that a match between her and Robert Tremaine would never happen. It was more a vision of what could never be.

He regarded her seriously. What if he had made a mistake? She responded to him physically, he knew that, but was that enough? What if she couldn't love him? He did not know if what he was about to do was wise or foolish, but he was about to find out.

He held out his hand. "Come, Emily."

Before they entered the library, he paused and turned towards her. "When we are with your uncle, I want you to let me do the talking and follow my lead."

Emily looked puzzled, as if wondering what on earth he could mean, but she agreed.

Her uncle had, by now almost emptied the decanter. "It took long enough, and by the look of you nothing has changed, but no matter, you shall come as you are," he muttered as he rose from the sofa. "Now get your cloak."

Robert took her hand and threaded it through the crook of his arm. His muscles tensed. "As I said to you earlier, Sir Clifford, Miss Conrad will not be leaving with you now or at any other time. She has just consented to become my wife."

There was a moment of absolute silence, broken only by the crackling logs in the fire grate.

"What are you talking about?" Sir Clifford's mouth was slack. "You cannot marry Emmy. She is already promised to another."

"It was not a formal betrothal I believe, more of an agreement between you and the other gentleman. In any case, Emily is free to marry the man of her choosing."

"She most certainly is not. As her guardian, I have chosen a suitable husband."

"Suitable for whom? You or your niece? The man you have chosen is a blackguard and a scoundrel, who, I'll wager, is marrying your niece for her money, and when he gets it, do you really suppose he will give you the share he has promised?"

"In any case, she will need my permission to marry. The terms of the will..." Beads of sweat were visible on the older man's forehead.

Robert knew his suspicion had hit home. "Ah yes, this will you have held over your niece's head, was the wording by chance 'when she decides to marry?'" Robert kept his tone mild. His experience as a soldier told him Sir Clifford was afraid. "Take your time to think, sir, or, if you cannot recall the exact wording, we shall send for your lawyer and read the document to make sure we have not missed anything. A will is a public document," he added helpfully.

He turned to Emily. 'Miss Conrad, would I be right in thinking that you have never actually seen this will your guardian sets so much store by?'

Emily nodded her head. "The lawyer read it after mama's funeral. I must confess, I did not take it in at that time, and uncle read some of it when he told me I was to marry Sir Richard, but, no I have never actually read it."

Sir Clifford's eyes raked over Emily before returning to Robert. "She, it says she, when she decides to marry," he spat out. "More interfering by my damned sister, believing that women should have some rights over their lives. Her stupid husband was no better." He rammed his hat on his head before turning back to Emily. "You have ruined me, girl. Ruined me."

Robert strode to the fire place and pulled on the cord. "No, she didn't. You did that and blamed everything and everyone but yourself. In your selfishness and greed, you were prepared to sacrifice this young woman to a man who would assist you to steal her fortune."

The door opened. "Ah, Hunter, please show Sir Clifford out."

"You have not heard the last of this. I shall go to my lawyer," Sir Clifford blustered.

"You can go to the devil for all I care, but if you attempt to contact Miss Conrad again, you will need more than a lawyer. Hunter."

"Yes, Your Grace?"

"If Sir Clifford attempts to enter the park, set the dogs on him."

"With pleasure, Your Grace."

Emily stood rooted to the spot. Her mind was in a whirl. Hours ago she did not even know her name. Now she had a life so complicated she could scarcely take it in.

Robert stood in front of her. "Are you all right? You're shaking." His eyes showed the concern she heard in his voice.

He led her to the sofa and she sat down before her knees gave way. He handed her a glass. "Drink this, it's brandy. It will make you feel better. Don't argue, Emily," he added as she opened her mouth to do just that.

She took a swallow, and, as before, coughed as the strong alcohol hit the back of her throat. "That," she gasped, "is just as disgusting as it was the first time you forced me to drink it."

"Ah, it's doing its work then. You're sparring with me." He grinned and took a large swallow from his own glass, before setting it down and sitting beside her.

Emily could have sworn that every nerve in her body was jangling as his muscled thigh brushed against hers. She took a deep breath. "I may never be able to thank you, Sir, for releasing me from my uncle. Now I know that I do not need his permission to marry, I am sure I can keep Ellerton going until my inheritance comes through."

He took her hands in his. The last thing he wanted was for her to disappear to Ellerton. "I suspect that it's not going to be quite as straightforward as that."

Her green eyes darkened. "What do you mean?"

"Your uncle is both a proud man and a desperate one. He needs his share of your fortune, and although he has gone without trouble tonight, I don't doubt but that he is already plotting as to how to restore his fortune."

"I don't understand."

"While you remain unmarried, you are not safe," he said bluntly.

"But how? My uncle has no hold over me. You said so yourself and he agreed."

Robert sighed, quickly deciding Emily needed to know the truth. "Your uncle and his friend planned for you to marry so that they could share your fortune. Now that avenue has been denied, they will be looking for another way to gain your inheritance."

She realized he was telling the truth. She had heard it from both of them before she had escaped.

"Emily, who is your next of kin?"

"Why, my uncle. I have no other kin." Her eyes widened with shock, "No, you surely don't think that my uncle would—"

"I'm afraid I do. While you remain single, were you to meet with an accident or were your uncle to abduct you and have you declared insane, he would regain the fortune that tonight eluded him."

Emily was not the sort of woman who fainted, but the enormity of Robert's words caused her to close her eyes for a moment as the room swam.

"Emily, open your eyes." Robert's voice was soft. "I have something to say and I want to know you are listening fully to me." Her green eyes searched his. "That is why we must marry as soon as possible, so I can protect you. Once you are married, your uncle will have no further claim on your fortune."

Emily's eyes widened. "You cannot marry me. I know you told that to my uncle to throw him off balance, but you are betrothed to Lady Arabella. Your engagement is to be announced tonight," she exclaimed.

Robert grimaced. "I assure you I am not betrothed to Arabella nor am I about to be."

"Then you do not love her?"

"Marriage is not about love," he said quietly. "Not where a dukedom is concerned. Marriage is about power and position, but no I do not love her." He wanted to add 'I love you,' but did not.

Her heart slowed and she lowered her eyes. "So what you are offering me is some kind of marriage of convenience?"

"Exactly, we will both benefit. You will be safe from your uncle and I shall gain a wife which will stop the endless processions of mammas throwing their daughters in my path, which is getting more than a little tedious."

Emily licked her lips. "Would you, I... have children?" Pink suffused her cheeks.

Her head was down so she did not see his smile. "Of course. One of the duties I expect of my wife is that she bears my children. It is our duty

71

to produce heirs." He placed a long finger under her chin and raised her head so that she could see him, "I promise you, Emily, we will make this work. I am a reasonable man. I want a wife who will take her place by my side, not three steps behind me."

"I would love to have children of my own," she confessed.

"Then do you agree to my proposal?"

There was a pause before she spoke. "But what if we do not suit? What if you grow tired of me or fall in love with someone? Will you then send me away or put me in an asylum?"

"I have not had a dull moment since you fell into this household. Somehow I do not think I will get tired or bored with you in several lifetimes, but if, and I am only saying this to give you an answer because I believe that the treatment you have received from your uncle makes it difficult for you to trust me, if there was an issue between us, we should sort it out as adults. If we could not," he added, "I would give you a generous income and home and you would of course retain your own money. You have my word on that. I will get my lawyer in tomorrow to draw up a contract to that effect so that you need have no fears. As to our not suiting...."

He drew her into his arms and kissed her until they were both breathless. "I do not think that will be a problem. Now, we have neglected our guests for long enough. Let us return to the ball. We have an announcement to make."

Chapter Thirteen

The ball was still in full swing. The chandeliers glittered. Dancers whirled while the older ladies sat around the edges, gossiping, drinking fruit punch, and fanning themselves. The single young men leaned against the walls waiting for a sign that the lady of their choice cared to acknowledge them. One or two couples had disappeared on to the terrace. Although the temperature was freezing, the prospect of a few moments of privacy was enough to tempt them. Some were married and others were just daring.

For propriety's sake, Robert and Emily entered separately. She was instantly whisked onto the dance floor. Robert headed towards his brother who was, as always, standing surrounded by a group of girls and laughing at something Lady Arabella said. Regardless of his mother's plotting, Robert had never intended to offer for Arabella, but he knew the damage that could be done when the gossips were disappointed.

As he approached, James his face turned serious. "Brother, we need a word. The terrace?" They excused themselves from ladies as James followed his brother with curiosity.

"I will be making an announcement tonight." Robert quickly outlined the events of the evening.

James whistled. "That's quite a story, Whitney, but are you sure about marriage? It's quite a step. Are you sure you want to be tied to someone you barely know for life? Miss Conrad is a lovely woman, but you know next to nothing about her."

"Most of our friends barely knew the women they married before the wedding and something tells me that life with Emily will be less than dull. In any case, it's decided. I am just about to make the announcement. We shall be married on Christmas Eve."

"Isn't that rushing things a bit?"

"Trust me, there are very good reasons," Robert said grimly. "Now let's go and light some fireworks."

As the brothers returned, they were surprised to see Emily and Arabella sitting at the edge of the room deep in conversation. Emily had been surprised when Arabella approached her to talk. Arabella received Emily's news about her memory with interest.

"You must forgive me, Miss Conrad. I fear I was most impolite. If your home is Ellerton Grange, then it would seem, our paths may cross from time to time, though I don't intend for Whitney and I to be buried in the country. He will be getting a society wife, not a country mouse when we marry."

Emily was horrified. Robert had proposed to her while Arabella clearly believed he was betrothed to her or almost.

Arabella narrowed her eyes. "Don't think you will ever wear those diamonds again," she hissed. "I don't know how you persuaded Robert to let you wear them tonight."

Summoning her spirit, Emily responded. "His grace very kindly loaned them to me for the evening."

Her head spun. How could Robert be prepared to announce his betrothal to her when he had clearly not settled matters with Arabella? Besides, how could she possibly contemplate tying herself in marriage to a man who had no scruples about the way he dealt with women? He was just like her uncle. He would use her as he wished while it suited him. Then he would dispose of her. He was worse because he had made her fall in love with him.

The arrival of the two brothers ended their tête-à-tête. James asked Emily to dance while Robert waltzed with Arabella. All the time Emily danced with James, she kept looking to see Arabella's face. She was amazed to see Arabella laugh and tap him with her fan as he escorted her back to James.

"It's time to light the fuse," Robert said to Emily with a grin, tucking her arm through his. He started to lead her to the small stage set up for the musicians, but she paused.

"Please, Your Grace," Emily whispered. "Please indulge me this one time. Don't make the announcement tonight. It's too much. I need some time to adjust to the idea."

He looked down at her. "Of course," he said quietly. "You are very pale. Are you feeling ill?" She heard the concern in his voice.

"I am just...overwhelmed," she said, struggling to find the right word.

"Very well, but I do not want our betrothal to remain secret. I—"

His mother who had appeared at his side cut him off. "Really Robert, have you no manners? Surely it is time you danced at least one dance with your mother."

He could have killed his mother. "Certainly, madam." He turned to Emily. "Please wait for me in the library," he whispered.

After that dance, his mother insisted he speak to several other guests because he had disappeared during the evening and had neglected his guests.

Emily moved, danced, smiled, and talked as though in a dream and fled as soon as she could. It was only now the prospect of marriage to Robert became real. She really had no idea why he had offered to marry her. He had said it was to protect her, but surely he could do that without marrying her? What if they did not suit? After all, they barely knew each other. As he said, most of the ton barely knew each other when they married, but then, most of the ton marriages were not happy. Once the wife had done her duty and provided heirs, most of them lived separate lives and she did not want that.

Although her parents' marriage had been all too brief, it had been a happy one, and she realised, that was what she wanted. She didn't want a marriage of convenience to a man who had offered out of a sense of duty, a man who, it seemed, despite what he said, would not scruple to put her aside when he tired of her, as he clearly had done with Lady Arabella. She wanted to love and be loved. She would tell him in the morning.

Emily stopped with her hand on the door knob. No, she wouldn't tell him in the morning because he wouldn't listen. Even if he did, he would brush aside her reasons and if that didn't work he would kiss her. He would use every weapon in his considerable arsenal until she agreed to his plans. She knew she would not, could not resist him. She would have to leave now, tonight, while there was a chance she could get a head start by several hours. She would take the boy's clothes she had borrowed, a saddle, and Apollo. It was only forty miles to London. She could make it in two days.

Emily had not really gone beyond this when she entered her room and found Lady Arabella sitting on her bed. "What are you doing here?" she said before she could stop herself.

"I saw you leave the ball and came to congratulate you," the other woman said coolly. "On your betrothal. I must confess I underestimated you." She smiled, but it did not reach her eyes. "Of course, Robert explained the betrothal will last a while so you can claim some sort of inheritance and then he will put you aside."

Emily took a deep breath, determined not to show how each word the other woman spoke cut into her like a knife. "Well you can keep your congratulations. I will not be marrying this duke or any other for that matter. However, I need your help."

Arabella's eyes narrowed. "Help?"

Realising Arabella would be delighted to get rid of her rival, Emily quickly outlined her plan. As she expected, the other woman was only too pleased to aid her.

Within fifteen minutes, Emily was once again attired as a boy with her riding habit and a few provisions, sneaked from the kitchen by Arabella in a hessian sack. Before departing, she penned a quick note explaining to Robert the reasons for her flight. She pressed the note into Arabella's hand. She willingly agreed to give it to Robert in the morning along with the jewels which Emily carefully returned to their box.

Arabella would tell Robert Emily was feeling unwell, had retired to bed, and would probably stay there until morning.

Soon, Arabella, who had apprised Lady Tremaine of Emily's plans, returned with a purse of money from Robert's mother with the message that she thought it was for the best. The two women would ensure Robert would not learn of her flight until later to give her a head start.

Fifteen minutes later, Emily and Apollo neared the edge of the park. In the distance, she could still hear the sound of laughter and music. She turned her horse and didn't look back.

Chapter Fourteen

The following morning, by the time the guests emerged for breakfast there was little evidence of the ball. The carpets had been re-laid and furniture returned to its usual places.

"So, Whitney, about this Miss Conrad. We are all intrigued," the elderly Countess of Harpington began. "She is quite the mystery. Who are her people? I don't recall her coming out. When did you meet her, Whitney?"

"Miss Conrad has been staying here while she recovered from a nasty head injury she sustained falling from her horse in the blizzard," Robert explained quickly.

The minute he mentioned the blizzard, the room came alive. Everyone had a story about it, and for the moment, Emily's history was forgotten.

Robert watched the door with growing alarm as the beautiful young woman he wanted by his side had not yet appeared. She had looked tense when he had last seen her in the ballroom, but Arabella had told him she had retired to bed with a headache.

The Countess of Harpington interrupted his reverie. "Well, Whitney, we must be on our way, but I shall look forward to your attendance at Harpington for the Old Year's Night Ball."

As though a signal had been given, the rest of the guests started to depart, and for the next two hours Robert was involved in wishing farewell to his guests.

As he was returning to the library, he caught sight of Alice coming down the stairs, and from the look of her, she had been crying. "What's the matter? Is Miss Conrad ill again?" he demanded.

Alice burst into tears. "She's not there, Sir. Her bed hasn't been slept in."

"What?" Robert was up the stairs, taking them two at a time with the small maid trailing in his wake. "She sent a message last night to say that she would sleep late this morning and not to wake her until noon, I thought she was just tired after the ball, but when I went in this morning her bed hadn't been slept in."

"What about her clothes?" Robert demanded as he threw open the door.

"Nothing's gone, Sir, except—"

"Except what, damnation?"

The little maid hesitated. "Her riding habit, Sir. The one she was wearing when she came here.''

"Son of a bitch," he growled, striding from the room.

Five minutes later, five grooms, Winters, and several stable lads were white faced as Robert interrogated them. "Do you mean to tell me that no-one saw Miss Conrad come into the stables, saddle her horse, and leave?"

Winters cleared his throat nervously. "There were so many horses to see to, Your Grace, what with house guests, coaches, visiting horses and their lads and the ball and such. When we came to see to them this morning, we assumed the young lady had gone out for a ride before breakfast."

Robert rubbed the back of his neck, quickly deciding the early morning ride story was less likely to raise curiosity both among the servants and his remaining guests. Perhaps he was being unreasonable. If he hadn't known his fiancée was about to bolt, why should the men before him?

"Very well, Winters. Arrange a full search of the park and beyond. As you say, Miss Conrad may have gone for an early morning ride and it's possible she may have met with an accident."

For the next two hours, careful questioning of the staff revealed no one had seen Emily since she told Arabella she was going to bed with a headache. He strode to the morning room where Arabella and his mother were enjoying a cup of hot chocolate.

"Ah, Whitney," his mother inclined her head. "Come in. This is a pleasant surprise. Did you want to join us for some chocolate or shall I ring for Hunter to bring some coffee?"

"Neither." He stalked over to the window and leaned his arm across it, rested his head, and stared bleakly out. "I suppose you have heard that Emily, Miss Conrad, has left."

"Naturally," Lady Tremaine responded, looking thoughtfully at her son over the rim of her cup. "I think you had better tell what you know, Arabella."

Arabella, who had been sitting demurely on the silk sofa, looked up, meeting Robert's gaze steadily. "I believe Miss Conrad left early this morning. I went to her room after rising because I was concerned about her." She hesitated.

"What?" Robert demanded.

"I found this." She held out her hand and Robert took the jewel box from her. "I didn't know what to do, so I came to talk to your mother."

"I gave them to Miss Conrad to wear at the ball. Did she leave no note, nothing to tell us where she was going?" He tossed the box on the table as Arabella shook her head, looking down.

"Open the box, Robert," his mother said quietly.

"I don't need to, mother. I know what is in it, the Whitney diamonds," he replied.

"No, they are not. That young woman you took in, fed, clothed, and presented to society has stolen them." She opened the box. "I knew from the start you could not trust her and this is how your kindness has been rewarded."

Robert looked at the empty box in disbelief. Every instinct he possessed screamed at him that this could not be true. Emily would not have stolen the jewels, but the evidence was clear. The jewels were gone and so was she. The thing he knew but his mother did not was that Emily desperately needed the money. Perhaps his mother was right. The woman had schemed since the moment she arrived. She had worked first on his sympathy and then on sexual attraction. God, he had been such a fool. He had allowed himself to be completely taken in, but she would not get away with it.

"Of course, she could be anywhere by now. She could have gone to Southampton and be on her way to the colonies," his mother suggested.

He pocketed the jewel box. "Miss Conrad, if that's even her name, will not get away with this. When I've finished with her, she'll beg to be taken to the colonies, and it won't be the Americas. Ladies." He bowed and strode from the room.

London. He would try there first. Emily would have to get rid of the jewels and London would be the best place to do that. Within the hour messages were sent to his agents in London to investigate discreetly anyone trying to sell the diamonds. Another trusted servant was dispatched to Ellerton Grange to discover whether she had gone there. Perhaps her uncle and she were in it together. Finally, he sent a message to have his town house ready. If she was in London, he wanted to be there to find her himself.

Piece by piece he erected a wall, ruthlessly crushing any memory, yet they continued to haunt him. Emily laughing in the snow, falling on top of him when they were skating, and most of all, melting in his arms when he kissed her. Fury and hatred were the two emotions he recognised now. It was not even the theft of the jewels that motivated him. He had handed her his heart on a plate. He had even offered her his name and she had betrayed him. That he could not forgive.

The messenger came back from Ellerton reporting that Sir Clifford was alone and drunk. Cropton had called off their agreement and he clearly had no idea where Emily was. That seemed to suggest that at least she was not in league with her uncle. It also suggested, however, that she was working alone. Two days later, he was on his way to London.

Chapter Fifteen

Ten months later, Robert was no nearer to finding Emily than he had been when he had discovered she was missing. His secretary stood in front of the desk in the study on Bruton Street.

"Where the devil is she? A woman can't just disappear from the face of the earth," Robert thundered.

"We're pretty sure she is still in the country, Your Grace." Burrows spoke with quiet assurance. The two men had known each other from their years in the army and Robert would have trusted Burrows with his life.

"Has she tried to sell the diamonds?"

"Not yet, Sir."

"Then what is she doing for money? According to the maid, she left with a set of boy's clothes and the riding habit she was wearing when we found her."

"A riding habit you say?" The secretary shuffled through the papers in the folder in front of him. "There's something here. A green riding habit, velvet with matching hat?'

Robert's heart lurched. "Yes, what is it man, quickly, this is the first thread of a clue we have had since she disappeared."

"One of my men visited the pawn brokers, of which there are a good many in London." he began. "A young woman answering the description of Miss Conrad pawned the riding habit sixteen days ago, though she did it under the name of Miss Emily Smith."

"That's her." Robert leaned forward.

"It's a common name, Sir."

"I know it's her." He could not help but be reminded of the night when they had decided on the name because she didn't know her own. He quashed the flare of emotion he felt. "Is there an address?"

"Yes, Sir." He consulted the paper again. "My man noted the young woman claimed to some sort of music teacher, pianoforte I think is what it says. We can go straight to the authorities and have them pick her up directly."

"No," Robert replied quickly, keeping his voice neutral, "I want to question her myself. I want her brought here, but I don't want her to have any warning, I don't want her to have time to work out some kind of plausible story." He was being irrational. A sensible man would leave it to the authorities and let justice take its course, but for some reason he could not articulate, he wanted to see her again one last time.

"Very well, Sir. If the young lady is purporting to be a teacher of the pianoforte, perhaps she could be persuaded to come here on the pretence of work. Maybe to tutor a young lady of the household."

"Brilliant, Burrows. We shall send her a note suggesting we have heard good reports of her work and Lord Basing wants her to tutor his young ward. Set it up."

"As you wish, Sir. Who, by the way, is Lord Basing?"

Robert smiled. "Me, one of the titles I inherited. That way, if Miss Smith asks questions there really is a Lord Basing."

"I imagine we shall have her in front of the authorities by the end of the week, if not before." He gathered his folder and left Robert alone.

A few minutes later, one of the passing maids was startled by the sound of glass shattering against the marble fireplace.

* * * *

True to his word, Burrows returned the following day to say Miss Smith would be coming to meet with her prospective employer the day after. "She seemed keen. I got the impression she has little money. Her lodgings are sparse."

"Then why hasn't she tried to sell the damned diamonds?" Robert snapped.

"Perhaps she knows she's being watched. But—"

"What?"

Burrows considered his words carefully. "I've seen many criminals, Your Grace, and I have to say, that young lady is something of an enigma. I could find nothing in her countenance that suggests she is anything other than innocent."

"Oh she does that very well, Burrows, that innocent look, but don't be fooled by it. The fact is both she and the jewels disappeared. What other explanation could there possibly be?"

"As you say, Sir, what other explanation could there be?"

* * * *

At precisely ten thirty, Miss Emily Smith knocked on the door of the house in Bruton Street. The butler's disapproval of her shabby appearance was palpable as he took her cape and bonnet and instructed her to wait.

Emily patted her hair nervously into place. She had scraped it into a tight bun at the nape of her neck, hoping that it would make her look older and therefore more likely to be hired. She did not sit on one of the silk covered chairs. She was both too nervous to sit and didn't want to soil the beautiful fabric with the dust that must be clinging to her gown. The walk from her Cheapside lodgings had been long.

When she had arrived in London, she had little idea of how she was to earn her living and keep out of sight until she could claim her inheritance. She had thought of trying to gain a position as a governess or paid companion, but the thought of running into Robert or one of the many people she had met at the Solstice Ball negated that idea.

She tried not to think of Robert at all, but he came unbidden into her thoughts. Sometimes she thought she saw him, but it was someone of the same height or colouring. She did not know what was worse, the thought of seeing him or of never seeing him. But the nights were worse. She lay in bed tossing and turning as he invaded her dreams, always just out of reach.

The butler returned. "The master will be with you shortly. Follow me, Miss." He led her down the hall into the drawing room.

The long elegant windows ensured light flooded the room. The pale green drapes complemented the array of sofas and chairs scattered around the room. The silence was broken by the ticking of an ormolu clock on the marble mantelpiece. A cheerful fire blazed in the grate, making the room feel warm in spite of the chill autumn wind. It would not be long before the first frosts of winter would be felt.

Emily's gaze was immediately drawn to the grand pianoforte at the end of the room. She turned to the butler but he had silently withdrawn. She did not know what to do. She should not sit down because she was a servant. She wandered over to the elegant instrument and ran her fingers over the keys deciding that if she was being interviewed as a tutor, her potential employer would probably want to hear her play. It would also calm her nerves. She sat down and was soon lost in the world of Mozart.

As her hands came down on the final triumphant chords of the sonata, her reverie was shattered by the sound of clapping. She whirled around from the keys and gasped. Sitting on one of the sofas was Robert, one long leg in front of him, the other booted ankle resting on top. Although he gave the impression of being totally relaxed, there was also something about him that reminded Emily of a cat ready to spring.

"Well played, Miss Conrad, or is it Miss Smith again. I confess I find it difficult to keep up with your different personas," he drawled.

Emily shot to her feet. The joy she had felt momentarily evaporated. Robert was not smiling. He was looking at her with barely veiled contempt and disgust. She had known he would be angry, but she had explained in her note the reasons for her flight. She had done it to save him from regretting his impulsive proposal and her even more impulsive acceptance. He should be grateful she had saved them from a loveless and unhappy marriage. If anyone had suffered for his impulsive actions, it was her.

His life had clearly gone on as before whereas hers was in tatters. She could not return to Ellerton and her uncle. She could not access funds from her solicitor who would inform her uncle where she was. Thus, she was the one reduced to living in two rooms in Cheapside and living in not so genteel poverty. There was nothing genteel about poverty. She straightened her spine. She would rather die than have Robert know how far she had fallen.

"I am confused, Your Grace." She smiled as she swept a low curtsey and raised her eyes to his, refusing to flinch at the coldness in his blue eyes. "I believed myself to be meeting Lord Basing to see if I might become music tutor to his ward." She kept her voice steady.

He said nothing, merely continuing to look at her as though she were a particularly interesting but unpleasant insect.

"I take it there is no work, no Lord Basing, and no ward," she said quietly. She curtsied again. Still he did not say anything. "In that case, I will take my leave, Your Grace." She turned towards the door.

"The hell you will," Robert said through gritted teeth. Before she had taken three steps, he was in front of her. "You have some explaining to do. Now we can either sit and do it in a civilised manner or the alternative, and I have to warn you, I am far from feeling civilised." Emily sat.

For several minutes Robert regarded her in silence. She had lost weight. Her gown was cheap and ill-fitting and her hair was scraped back which had the effect of highlighting her cheekbones and making her eyes huge in her delicate face. He frowned.

Selling the jewels would give her more than sufficient to live in some degree of comfort. Why had she not sold them immediately? She was not stupid. She would have known that selling them immediately and going abroad would have been her best chance of getting away with the theft. Yet she had not. She had stayed in London and was sitting opposite him with every air of innocence.

He gave himself a mental shake. He had trusted that air of innocence before. If the jewels were at her lodgings, they would be in his hands within the hour. As soon as she had left to come here Burrows and his men had entered and were searching her rooms. If the jewels were found, Burrows would return with them and Miss Emily Conrad would be handed over to the authorities. From there she would be hanged or transported, either way he would be rid of her.

"Your Grace," Emily began, unable to stand the silence any longer, "I am truly sorry for leaving Charleton so abruptly. I realise I should have had the courage to speak to you in person, but I did not."

"Spare me the innocent act, Miss Conrad." His voiced sliced through her like a knife. "I'm not interested. Just tell me what you have done with them."

Her eyes shot to his in puzzlement. "Done with what?"

"I believe I have already established the fact that you are a liar as well as a thief, Miss Conrad. If you want to save your pretty little neck, I would suggest that you tell me where the Whitney diamonds are and fast. I am rapidly beginning to run out of patience."

Emily surged to her feet. "You think I stole the Whitney diamonds?" she gasped.

His hands closed on her arms. "I don't think it, I know it. You were the last one to have the diamonds. When you left, the diamonds left with you. Now I am prepared to draw a line under the whole disastrous thing if you confess to what you have done and return the diamonds. If not, you will be handed over to the authorities."

Emily went numb. How had it come to this? The man, who a few short months ago had nursed her back to health and even offered her the protection of his name, now thought she had stolen from him. She had left him so he would not feel under any obligation to fulfil his promise, which she felt sure he would have regretted in the cold light of day.

"Let me go please, and don't touch me ever again," she said quietly. He dropped his hands to his sides.

"I don't know where your diamonds are because I did not take them. The only things I took were the boy's clothing I had borrowed before, which I will return to you, and my own clothes. If you truly believe I stole the jewels, then you must refer me to the authorities. Do what you will but I would like to leave now."

She could have explained she had left the diamonds and a note with Arabella, but she didn't think Robert would believe her. He had already acted as judge and jury, and she couldn't prove her actions. Arabella would deny it. Why would he believe a woman he barely knew above one he had known all his life? The thing that cut deepest was that Robert was willing to believe her guilty in the first place. The poverty she now faced as she hid from her uncle was nothing to the betrayal she felt by Robert.

He did not attempt to stop her as she walked towards the door, her head was held high, but he could almost feel the effort she was making to retain her dignity. Every cell in his body screamed at him to stop her, to throw himself at her feet and beg her to stay, but he crushed his feelings. Cold logic and evidence could not be ignored. She had worn the diamonds and when she had left Charleton, the diamonds had gone with her. He didn't bother to stop her. Burrows had someone watching her, she would not escape him a second time.

At the door she paused. "I think Your Grace would be well advised to look to some of your guests about the diamonds. I am sorry our friendship should end like this, Sir. I will not contact you again, and I would ask that you do not contact me. If you decide to bring me before the authorities, I cannot prove that I did not take the diamonds. All I can say is that I give you my word." There was a quiet click as she closed the door behind her.

Chapter Sixteen

Within ten minutes of her departure, Burrows was sitting opposite Robert in his study. "My men went through her lodgings with a fine tooth comb. The diamonds are not there."

"Could she have hidden them somewhere else?'" Robert suggested.

The other man's eyes narrowed as he considered the possibility. "I suppose so, but in my experience a thief would want to keep something of great value somewhere they could both keep an eye on it and where they can access it easily."

"You're sure you couldn't have missed them?"

Burrows smiled. "There was little enough to search, Your Grace, a few items of clothing, nothing of value. Her landlord said she had paid for three months lodgings in advance and has repeated the process each time."

"Did he say anything else?"

"She arrived around Christmas time with a horse. She asked how much the room was and came back later that day with the money. He hasn't seen the horse since. A fine beast by all accounts."

"She sold the horse? I cannot believe Miss Conrad would sell her horse. She loved Apollo." Robert spoke partly to himself.

Burrows took a deep breath. "Your Grace, I don't believe you are quite aware of the depth to which Miss Conrad has fallen. She is living in two rooms in Cheapside. I have to tell you, Sir, I would not like my daughter to even walk through those streets, let alone have to live there. Miss Conrad is a lady. Quite how she is coping with living among thieves, vagabonds, and women of the streets, I cannot imagine."

"The more I hear about Miss Conrad, the less I think I know her," Robert said thoughtfully. He could not get the image of her face out of his mind. She had not looked guilty, puzzled and resigned, but not guilty. And hurt, he conceded ruefully.

They were interrupted by a messenger for Burrows. He read it quickly and looked up smiling. "Good news, Your Grace, one of my men thinks he has found the diamonds. Apparently a young woman sold them to a jeweller in Hatton Garden this morning. He bought them apparently in good faith. My man is bringing him here with the jewels."

The jeweller was clearly terrified of Robert, Burrows, and the risk of being arrested for buying stolen property. He laid the jewels out on Robert's desk. "I swear I did not know they were stolen, Your Grace. The young woman said she needed the money to pay her gambling debts."

"And you believed that?"

"You would be surprised, my lord, how many young wives sell and buy back their jewels for that purpose," he replied, dabbing at his forehead with a less than clean handkerchief.

"The young woman,"—Burrows leaned forward—"describe her. Would you say she was a gentlewoman?"

"Definitely, Sir."

"Dressed in black? Auburn hair? Green eyes?"

"No, Sir. The young lady was richly dressed in pale blue. I remember because it matched the colour of her eyes. She kept her hood on, but her hair was fair, like the colour of spun gold. I am a jeweller, Sir, and we notice colour," he apologised.'

"Are you sure of that?" Burrows demanded.

"Quite sure, Sir."

"And would you recognise this young woman were you to see her again?"

The jeweller mopped his brow again. "Yes, Sir, the young lady was not one a person would forget in a hurry."

"You say you bought the jewels in good faith. What made you realise the jewels were stolen?" Robert prompted.

The man looked embarrassed. "I'm sorry to say, Your Grace, it was Old Ted. He's worked for us since my grandfather's time, possibly even before that. He seems to be part of the building. He recognised them, but I

89

didn't take much note. Old Ted's not so reliable as he was and his mind wanders a bit. He said his grandfather made them for a duchess but he couldn't remember who. It was only when your man came in and asked about the diamonds that I put the two things together. I wouldn't want Your Grace to think ill of me or my business. I run a respectable business."

"I'm sure you do," Burrows replied. "His Grace has no interest in reporting this to the authorities at this time and would appreciate your discretion in the matter."

Robert's mind was only half on the conversation playing out in front of him. The jeweller had not described Emily. She was not the one who had sold the diamonds. He drew in a breath remembering her parting words to look to some of his other guests. He knew which woman the jeweller had described.

After seeing the jeweller out, Burrows returned to find Robert dashing off note after note. "See that these are delivered as a matter of urgency. My mother and my brother were coming here in a few weeks anyway for the start of the season. It just means they will have to bring their visit forward."

Burrows cleared his throat. "What of the young lady? He did not describe Miss Conrad. Indeed, while the jewels were being sold, Miss Conrad was here, unless of course she was working with another. If not, it would seem we have sorely misjudged her."

Robert looked at the other man with anguish in his eyes. "I have misjudged her, Burrows. I acted as judge, jury, and executioner, believing the worst of her because I was angry that she had left without a word."

"What explanation did Miss Conrad give when you questioned her about the theft?" Burrows asked.

"None," Robert answered. "She denied taking the jewels and left. I will never forget the look on her face when I accused her, but I will make it up to her." *Or die trying,* he added silently. He picked up his coat and started towards the door. "Now, give me Miss Conrad's address."

"'Are you sure this is wise, Sir? I can have one of my men bring her here directly."

"Thank you, Burrows, but I must do this myself."

"What of the other young woman, Sir; the one who sold the jewels?"

Robert paused for a moment. "I'll deal with that matter later. For now, the most important thing is to get Emily back here safely."

The ride to Cheapside was swift. He instructed the carriage to follow him in the hope that Emily would agree to accompany him back to Bruton Street. Wide streets gave way to smaller streets and the nearer he got, the shabbier the streets became and the shabbier they were, the more they teemed with humanity. Unwashed, ragged children played in a muddy puddle at the edge of the street. A group of men played cards on a barrel outside one of the many taverns. Two women argued over a scrap of cloth, egged on by a small crowd that gathered to watch the entertainment. Three or four dogs ran loose, chased by a gang of older boys.

The many alleys gave anyone the opportunity to pounce on the unwary. It must be a haven for cutpurses and thieves. Emily was living here, and it was his fault. If he had not pressed her, if he had proposed properly rather than making it sound like some kind of business deal where he was doing her an immense service, then she would not be here. After their last meeting, he wondered whether she would agree to see him at all.

His fear for Emily's safety increased when he knocked at the door of the tenement. It eventually swung open to reveal a shifty looking man who could have been anything from thirty to sixty. His hair was sparse and hung in greasy clumps; his face was pock-marked and scarred, partly through disease and partly from some kind of wound.

He eyed Robert with equal suspicion. "What d' ye want? This is a respectable 'ouse, there ain't no rough trade 'ere."

"I'm looking for a woman," Robert began.

"Yer in the wrong place, mate. I told yer, this is a respectable 'ouse. You want a woman, try George Street." The man made to close the door.

"You misunderstand. I am looking for a particular young woman." Robert planted his boot firmly on the doorstep and his shoulder on the frame.

"Who?"

"Miss Smith."

The man laughed. "They're all called Miss Smith, yer lordship."

Robert squelched the desire to take the man by the throat and shake the information out of him. "I am looking for Miss Emily Smith and I am reliably told she is renting two rooms in this place. Now either tell me where she is or get out of my way so I can find someone who knows."

"A di'nt say A di'nt know," the man replied sulkily. Robert raised an eyebrow.

"She does live 'ere, but she's out an' she won't be back 'til after dark," he said grudgingly.

Robert gathered the final thread of his patience. "Then where is she?"

The man looked Robert up and down, "Now the question I asks meself is, what's a fine gentleman such as you, milord, doing in a place like this, and what business does 'e 'ave with our Miss Smith?"

"That is none of your business."

"Then get your boot out of my door, milord. I'll tell Miss Smith there was a gentleman to see her, but we looks after our own 'ere an' we ain't 'avin' no gentleman upsettin' 'er and puttin' 'er back in the terrible state she was in when she come 'ere."

"What do you mean terrible state?"

"Miss Smith was as innocent as a newborn babe when she come 'ere. If we hadn't looked after 'er, she would 'ave soon been parted from 'er money. It's my belief some gentleman done 'er wrong," he added, looking fiercely at Robert. "If you ask me, she 'ad a broken 'eart, that's what and I ain't about to let it 'appen again."

Robert looked at the man with a new sense of respect, although a good head shorter than him, the man looked as though he would have fought a duel with him if he must. He was also thankful this man had been prepared to look after Emily when he had failed her.

"I promise you I mean no harm to Miss Smith, but I need to speak with her and, when I have finished, I am hoping Miss Smith will return with me so that I can take care of her."

The man's eyes narrowed suspiciously. "What do yer mean? Take care of her? She ain't no fly-by-night, deserves a ring on her finger does Miss Smith. She ain't the sort to be a rich man's mistress even though she ain't got no money. You rich fellers make me sick, takin' advantage of a poor young woman—"

He would have gone on but Robert interrupted him, "Look, I have no intention of making Miss Smith my mistress if that's what you mean. I want to marry her." He surprised himself. Robert rarely discussed his feelings with his own brother, let alone a complete stranger who neither knew nor, it would seem, cared that Robert was a peer of the realm.

The man peered closely at Robert. "Marry 'er. You'd better or I'll 'ear of it and I know people," he added darkly.

"So do I," Robert replied drily.

"You'd better come in then. You can wait in Miss Smith's rooms. There ain't nothing worth stealin' any way." He moved to the side to allow Robert through into the dingy hall.

"I can assure you I have no intention of stealing anything," Robert heard himself replying even though the idea was ludicrous.

"I knows that, Your Grace, that's why I'm a-lettin' you in."

Robert paused mid-stride. This man had known who he was from the beginning but was unimpressed by power and position. He could not help but smile.

"Respect is earned, Your Grace. It ain't given because a man 'appens to be born in the right bed," he said as he selected a key and inserted it into the lock.

"I have a feeling that in some quarters you could be considered a very dangerous man."

"A man with ideas is often considered dangerous." The landlord pushed the door open. "This is Miss Smith's gaff."

Chapter Seventeen

The last thing Emily felt like was going to the church, but she knew the women would be waiting for her. Desperate for something to occupy both her time and mind when she arrived in London and encouraged by the vicar, a young Rev Dennis, she had started an evening class for women to teach them reading and writing.

The first week only two women came. They sought shelter from the cold they said and weren't really interested in learning,

"Ain't much call for readin' and writin' when yer flat on yer back," Annie, the older one, said. They both cackled. They appreciated the warmth and returned the following week bringing two more women with them.

After five weeks, about fifteen women attended and some of them could now write their own name. One or two had begun to read from the simple books the vicar had managed to obtain. They also formed a choir.

One time when they arrived, they caught Emily practising on the pianoforte. She then realised she could use their interest in music and started to set the alphabet to tunes.

Before long, the women brought their children and some men also attended. They enjoyed the reading and writing, but they loved singing. When Rev Dennis suggested they might stay longer to sing, Emily found herself leading a choir. Rev Dennis always escorted Emily to her lodgings and made it clear he took pleasure in doing so.

Once a week, the dark, solemn walls of St Mary's resounded with the voices of a choir no one had seen the likes of before. The women wore scarlet dresses with feathers in their hair and more flesh showing than perhaps Rev Dennis was comfortable with. It amused Emily to see the poor man blush so easily. The women took pleasure in making him flush to the roots of his hair.

The men often arrived after a day's work, some with aprons over their patched and mended trousers, quickly stuffing their hats into their pockets as they entered the church. Many of them had not been in a church since they were young. The children wore whatever their parents could find. Some came in clothes they were growing into and some in clothes they were growing out of, but rarely in something that fitted them and always patched sometimes to the point where it was impossible to tell what the original garment looked like.

Once she got there, Emily was glad she had come. It would have been all too easy to hide in her room. At least here she found diversion and some satisfaction in knowing that in some small way she was making a difference.

The choir began to sing in the simple harmonies she devised. She received a good deal of teasing, but once she grew accustomed to their roughness, she realised they not only meant no harm, but they looked out for each other. They certainly looked out for her.

One week, as she walked home with her small supply of provisions, two young men, somewhat the worse for wear, accosted her. They took hold of her string bag and reticule. Then, two of the men from the choir appeared from an alley and sent her would-be attackers on their way with a couple of sharp punches and more than a few choice words ringing in their ears.

All in all, Emily had matured considerably in the weeks she had lived in Cheapside. She learned a great deal about the lives of ordinary poor folk and vowed that when she came into her inheritance, she would do something practical to help them. She now knew they needed something more than 'the lady of the manor' distributing charity. They needed schools and medicines and the chance to earn enough to feed their children and keep a decent roof over their heads. From her privileged position, she was guilty, as were most of her class, of thinking the poor were a race apart. Now that she had lived among them and gotten to know them, she realised they were no different from the rich. It was an accident of birth, no more, that some were born with so much and some with so little.

As she wearily pushed open the door to her lodgings, her mind was on the choir. Rev Dennis was keen for them to perform at the Advent service. Emily realized that although in many ways a callow young man, he recognised the potential for his career and had already invited the Bishop. If it went well, he might be given a parish with a better living, though of course he had said nothing of this to Emily. Nonetheless, she understood when he suggested the choir should be ready to perform in public. To her surprise, they had been keen to do so.

Although her room was cold tonight, Emily knew she could not afford to light a fire. Now that she had no prospect of work with Lord Basing, she would have to eke out her meagre money still further until she could find a pupil. She lit the candle and the shadows receded.

"Thank God for that. I was beginning to think I was going to freeze to death in the dark," a familiar voice drawled.

Emily whirled around. "What are you doing here, Your Grace? I thought we said all we had to say to each other this morning. Now please leave."

"I'm afraid I can't do that, Miss Conrad," Robert replied firmly.

"Very well, then I shall." Emily whirled around.

She had taken two steps before Robert was in front of her. "I'm afraid I cannot let you do that either, my love." He held her arms in a vice-like grip, even though his voice was soft.

Something in Emily snapped. "Don't you dare 'my love' me. I never want to see you again. You arrogant, selfish, manipulative—"

"Bastard?" he suggested helpfully.

Emily glared at him. "Let me go, Your Grace, or I shall scream and there are people who will come to help."

Robert grinned. "I have no doubt my dear that a veritable army of besotted young men will materialise to defend your honour, and many of them would take an inordinate amount of pleasure in clubbing me to death. If I let you go, will you promise to at least listen to what I have to say?"

Emily regarded him with suspicion. "If I listen, do you promise to leave and never contact me again?"

Robert almost groaned. In truth he could not blame her. He had almost seduced her, proposed a marriage of convenience when she thought he was almost betrothed to someone else, and then accused her of being a thief. No wonder she looked at him as though he were a particularly unpleasant insect she wanted to crush beneath her foot.

"If, after I have spoken, you feel the same way, then of course I will respect your wishes," he said mildly, his brain working overtime. Just the sight of her made his blood sing. He could not tolerate the thought of failing.

He slid his hands down her arms, pressing her hands with the lightest touch before he thrust his into his pockets to stop himself from hauling her into his arms and kissing her until she complied. He had enough experience with women to know he could manipulate her sexually, but he instinctively knew that would be a disaster. Emily had to come to him in complete trust and of her own volition. If he took advantage of her innocence and manipulated her, she would resent him. He had to be honest with her. He wanted their relationship to work on every level, not just in his bed.

He took a steadying breath. "I have come to apologise, Miss Conrad. I fear I have misjudged you. I do not believe you stole the diamonds," he began.

"Thank you, Your Grace. I accept your apology. Now please leave." She moved to open the door.

"No you don't." He placed his boot firmly at the base of the door. "You promised to listen," he reminded her.

"I have listened and accepted your apology. What more is there to say? Goodbye, Your Grace."

He was relieved. For the first time she looked him straight in the eye and he saw the fire and spirit he thought his actions had doused.

"Oh there's plenty to say, Miss Conrad. You just need to be a little patient."

"Patient? If I were any more patient where you're concerned, I should expect to be made into a saint," she snapped back.

Despite the precarious nature of their relationship, he could not help but grin. This was the real Emily, his Emily. "Miss Conrad, I am conscious of the fact that since the ball I have made many grave mistakes, but I want you to know my proposal of marriage was made with sincerity."

"I believe you," she replied quietly.

It wasn't the words that caused the ripple of fear to shudder through him. It was the toneless, lifeless quality in her voice.

"I do believe you. You were prepared to offer me your name so I would have protection from my uncle and Your Grace would have a wife and heirs." He began to relax. "Then you would put me aside and take up your own life again," she finished.

"Emily," Robert reared back, "what are you talking about. What is this about being put aside?"

She looked at him with derision. "Please don't insult my intelligence, Your Grace. It was made quite clear to me that this was to be a marriage of convenience and once you had your heir I was to be set aside and you could take up your life again. A man of your means would have found a way to be rid of an unwanted wife."

Arabella, damn her. He would bet his life on it that she was behind this. He took Emily's hands in his. This was worse than he thought. If he could not persuade her to believe him and fast, he would lose her, forever.

"Please, Emily, listen to me. I know I have done you a great disservice, but let me assure you I had, nor did I ever have any intention of putting you aside. You have to believe me."

Emily looked down at their hands, "I know Your Grace made a generous offer. I also believe that when you thought over it you began to regret it."

"Never," he insisted. "I have never, nor could I ever, regret my proposal to you. Damn it all, Emily, I am in love with you. If you don't marry me, I think I shall go mad."

Her head shot up, her eyes wide with shock. "I don't understand. You think I am a liar and a thief."

"No, Emily, I think I am a fool, the biggest fool in the country. I was angry that you had left without speaking to me and the missing jewels gave me a focus for my anger. The only thing you are guilty of stealing," he added softly, "is my heart."

"You love me?" she said. "Truly?" She would not risk her heart again.

"I truly do," he confirmed. "Please forgive me. I have been a fool, an arrogant fool. I have hurt you but I promise I intend to spend the rest of my life making up for it."

For the first time she smiled, but he was perturbed to see tears shimmering in her eyes. "Oh, my love, I am so sorry." He traced a tear as it fell down her cheek. He could bear it no longer. He needed to feel her in his arms.

It was her undoing. "I couldn't bear it,"—she sobbed into his chest— "when you thought I was a thief."

"I know, I know." He stroked her hair. "I'm a fool, a jealous, stubborn fool, that's why you must marry me. You need to save me from myself."

"I shouldn't have run away like that," she conceded.

"It doesn't matter. It's in the past. What is important now is what happens in the future, our future. Please, my darling, put me out of my misery and tell me you will consent to be my bride."

"I don't recall that you have actually asked me, Your Grace," she replied with the impish grin he adored.

"Minx." He grinned, abruptly releasing her and going down on one knee. "Emily, Miss Conrad, would you do me the very great honour of becoming my wife?"

"If you're sure…"

"I have never been more sure of anything in my life," he said solemnly.

"Then yes, Your Grace, I shall marry you."

"Thank God," he muttered dragging her into his arms.

Chapter Eighteen

Within minutes they were in his carriage, Emily's hand enfolded in his. "I lost you once. I have no intention of losing you again."

On the way back to Bruton Street, he listened as she told him of her experience in London, of the class she taught, and the choir she had formed. "The vicar wants them to perform in the Advent service. I should very much like to finish what I started. The music means so much to them."

Robert shook his head. "No, Emily, it isn't safe. You would be a great prize for cutpurses and footpads."

She raised her eyebrows. "I shall be perfectly safe. The people know me."

"As my wife, you will promise to obey me."

"Are you forbidding me to visit my friends in Cheapside?"

Robert sensed this was an important question. "No, I am not forbidding you. I am merely pointing out that as a Duchess, you will be considered more of a target than a penniless music teacher in a frankly hideous gown."

Emily looked down at her gown. "The gown is hideous," she conceded. "As your duchess, I will promise to obey you. Unless—"

Now it was Robert's turn to raise an eyebrow. "Unless?"

Emily gave him her sweetest smile. "Unless your commands are obviously unreasonable," she countered.

He burst out laughing. "You are going to be the death of me," he muttered before he pulled her onto his lap and kissed her soundly.

When they arrived back at Bruton Street, they were met by servants unpacking. The coach bearing his mother had arrived and various carts with trunks and boxes were being unloaded and carried into the house.

"Oh no," Emily gasped. "I cannot meet Lady Tremaine looking like this."

"Like what?" Robert said taking in her slightly flushed cheeks, sparkling eyes, and moist lips.'

Her hands were trying to tidy her hair which had come loose from the tight chignon, "I look like—"

"A woman who has been soundly kissed by the man who cannot wait to make her his." His voice dropped, "In every sense of the word."

Her flush deepened. "Please, Your Grace, you shouldn't say such things."

He grinned at her, enjoying her discomfort. "Miss Conrad, I shall say and do a great deal more when we are man and wife." He handed her down from the carriage. Emily was relieved to see Alice waiting by the front door.

"It seems your luck is in. No doubt my mother will have gone to rest after her journey so Alice can take you to your room and attend to you. That gown is to be burned. I don't want anything to remind us of these last few wasted months. Tomorrow you will go to the modiste and order a whole new wardrobe. I want everyone to see the beautiful woman I am to marry dressed as she should be in the finest London has to offer."

Emily rolled her eyes. "I am flattered by your description, Your Grace, but I know I am not a beauty. My uncle said that in a good light I am tolerable at best."

Robert could not believe his ears. "Your uncle,"—he gritted his teeth, wanting to throttle the man afresh—"would not recognise beauty if it bit him on the arse."

Emily giggled. "Is this the kind of language I can expect to hear from now on, Sir? Such is not befitting the ears of a lady."

He roared with laughter. He could not remember the last time he had felt so happy. For the first time, he felt complete.

"Imp. I can guarantee that you will hear, see, and do things that will make you blush from the top of your head to the tips of your toes, and I intend to see all of it," he whispered in her ear, grinning as she blushed and ran up the stairs into the house.

* * * *

Alice was delighted to see her. "Oh Miss, I am so glad you're back where you belong. It wasn't the same without you," she said as she styled Emily's hair, teasing a few tendrils from the chignon. "Even Lady Tremaine missed you."

"I'm sure she did," Emily replied wryly.

"Lady Tremaine is looking forward to meeting you again," Alice said shyly. "She said that if you can make her son happy, then she will welcome you to the family."

"But what of Lady Walmesly?" Emily could not help blurting out.

Alice frowned. "I was sent to look after Lady Walmesly after you left, Miss, but she left as soon as his grace left for London, and good riddance too." Noticing, Emily's disapproval she unrepentantly added, "Well she's a nasty piece of work, Miss. I know I shouldn't speak ill of my betters, but that's the honest truth."

"Well, I suppose it's always a good thing to be honest," Emily responded with a smile.

"And she has more clothes than she knows what to do with," Alice continued, warming to her theme. "She left three silk shawls and two chemises as well as her reticule from the ball. Lady Tremaine said we should be seeing her in London so we brought them with us, see." She pulled them out of the trunk.

The shawls were indeed of the finest silk, and Emily recalled the tiny jewelled reticule which matched Arabella's ball gown. She held it up and admired it as the tiny jewels sparkled in the light. The clasp had come open in the trunk. As Emily went to close it, she noticed something inside. Almost without thinking, she drew out four torn pieces of paper. The remains of the note she had written to Robert explaining why she was leaving and which Arabella had promised to deliver to him. She looked at Alice.

"Nasty piece of work," Alice repeated.

A knock on the door interrupted them. Without waiting for an answer, Lady Tremaine entered with a determined look on her face. A nod was all Alice needed to excuse herself.

"I have come to apologise, Miss Conrad," she began.

"Please, Lady Tremaine, there's no need."

"Forgive me, Miss Conrad, but there is every need. I behaved in a most unpleasant way towards you." She waved her hand, dismissing Emily's protest.

"Arabella seemed a good choice and frankly Robert didn't seem to care whom he married. I see now that not only would they never have made each other happy. They would have actually made each other unhappy," she admitted.

Emily smiled shyly at the older woman. "I promise I shall do everything I can to make him happy."

Lady Tremaine returned the smile. "You will not have to try hard. I have never seen my son happier than when he is with you. I know I do not deserve it, but please forgive me, my dear." She held out a hand.

Emily's smile became a grin. "I hope you and I will be friends." She ignored the older woman's hand and hugged her. The formidable Lady Tremaine was no longer so formidable. "I should like nothing better," she said.

"Then tomorrow, we shall enjoy spending Robert's money. The season is in full swing and we must act swiftly to ensure you become its toast, though thankfully you have already landed your duke and do not need to go through the marriage mart."

Emily's smile faded. She wanted to be Robert's wife more than she had ever wanted anything, but she had not really considered the social obligations she would be under as a duchess.

The older woman patted her hand. "Don't look so worried, my dear. You charmed both of my sons with very little effort, and I shall be on hand to launch you. Trust me, Miss Conrad; you will be the talk of the ton before the month is out."

Chapter Nineteen

True to her word, Lady Tremaine took charge of Emily's launch into society. The following morning, they went to Madame Chantelle's. They examined bolt after bolt of fabric as Emily was measured for morning dresses, day dresses, walking dresses, afternoon dresses, carriage dresses, ball gowns, and riding habits, each with matching accessories, hats, boots, gloves and reticules, to say nothing of a range of capes and pelisses.

"Are you sure one person needs quite so many clothes?" she asked her future mother-in-law as they paused to take tea.

"Of course. Robert gave me strict instructions that nothing is to be scrimped."

"I don't think Madame is from France," Emily whispered.

"I don't think she's even seen the white cliffs of Dover, let alone France," Lady Tremaine smiled. "She pretends she's French so she can charge ridiculous prices and we pretend to believe her because she really is the best in London. That, by the by is one of the most important lessons you need to learn about London society—no-one is apparently who they seem."

Emily was intrigued. "I'm not sure I understand."

"Well,'" Lady Tremaine began, casting her glance around the room. "Take that young woman over there in the ivory carriage dress."

Emily's gaze followed and saw an exquisitely beautiful young woman sitting alone drinking tea. "Who is she?"

"That is Lady Carolina Hartnell. She is not received in polite society because her husband fought a duel over her. A foolish young man saw her driving in the park and wrote her a love poem. When her new husband found it, he called him out."

"What happened?"

"I believe both of them suffered minor injuries."

"Had Lady Hartnell encouraged the young man?"

"Not as far as I can tell. Apparently he saw her and fell in love with her. I don't think she even knew about him until after the duel."

"It seems most unfair that her reputation is the one in tatters when it was the action of the young man and her husband that caused the scandal," Emily said.

Lady Tremaine looked at her future daughter-in-law with respect. "When I first heard some of your ideas about the female race, I must confess I thought them to be absurd, but on closer consideration, I begin to concede you may have a point. However, as things stand, the best advice I can give you is to let your husband believe he is managing things. A clever wife usually gets her way if she knows how these things are done."

Emily's face clouded. She could not help but remember how unsuitable Lady Tremaine had thought her. How could she be the wife Whitney deserved, let alone his duchess? She had no template, no pattern. Her memories of her own mother were faded and, although she knew her parents had married for love, she had seen no examples of it.

"Is there something wrong, my dear?" Lady Tremaine enquired. "Did I say something to upset you?"

Emily shook her head. "Of course not. It's just that I am concerned I shall disappoint Whitney, I do not know how to be a wife, and I certainly do not know how to be a duchess like..." She stopped.

"Like Arabella?" Lady Tremaine said, softly. Emily nodded.

Lady Tremaine took a deep breath. "Miss Conrad, Emily, you are to put Arabella quite out of your mind. I must confess I sorely misjudged you, and I was most certainly misguided in my judgement of Arabella." She paused and patted Emily's hand.

"Arabella was spoiled and indulged as a small child and it has done nothing to give her character. She decided, encouraged by her parents and I must confess I thought it a good idea at the time, that she would be a good match for Whitney and set about making sure it would happen. She chased off every other female she saw as a rival. Whitney led his own life, and I suspect, until he met you, he would have settled for a ton marriage of convenience and continued as he had before. However, with her last trick, Arabella went too far."

"Too far?" Emily echoed.

"Why stealing the Whitney diamonds and placing the blame on you of course."

Emily stared at Lady Tremaine. "Arabella stole the diamonds?"

Lady Tremaine's eyes darkened. "I have just had a most uncomfortable meeting with my son and a Mr. Burrows. It emerged that, instead of returning them to Whitney as you asked, she came up with the scheme of stealing them and buying a passage to the Americas in your name so the blame would fall on you. She tried to get rid of them but the jeweller recognised them. In any case, Whitney's men were already making enquiries all over London. When I saw Arabella the morning after the ball, she had already concocted the story of the missing jewels and I believed her."

"What of Arabella now?" Emily asked.

Lady Tremaine paused. "At the moment, Whitney wants to report her to the authorities and let justice take its course."

"He cannot do that," Emily cried.

"Why not? It is no less than she deserves."

"Were Arabella to go to court, the scandal would destroy her and her parents. It would not only destroy Arabella's family, it would besmirch the Whitney name and Robert would also lose his brother."

Lady Tremaine looked mystified. "James? What has James to do with this?"

"James is in love with Arabella and I think, she with him."

Had the topic not been so serious, Emily thought she would have laughed out loud. Lady Tremaine looked as though she had swallowed a spoon.

"James and Arabella," she said thoughtfully. "I had not considered that."

Emily was already on her feet. "Come, we must go quickly."

"To what purpose?"

"To stop Robert making a bigger mistake than the one Arabella made," Emily replied.

Lady Tremaine laid a hand on her arm, "You were concerned earlier in this conversation that you would not make a good wife or duchess to Whitney. Let me tell you now, my dear, that he is lucky to have you, and so am I."

Chapter Twenty

Robert sat in his study, reading a report from his lawyer regarding land he had recently purchased. Actually, his mind was on Emily. He quickly ran through his supply of memories. Emily smiling at the absurd names they had suggested when she had lost her memory. Dancing with him at the ball, her eyes shining. Laughing as she pretended to be a stable lad and giggling when she fell on top of him as he taught her to skate.

When he ran out of memories, he began on fantasies. The way he would kiss her on their wedding night and how he would remove every stitch of her clothing and lay her on his bed so he could feast his eyes on her glorious body. His body tightened at the thought but he continued. He would kiss her. Starting at the top of her head, he would work his way down. Her eyes first, her nose, the little dimple in her cheek, and ending with her delicious lips. He had already tasted them, but he wanted more. How he longed to touch her breasts, to feel them full in his hands, and to tease their sensitive buds to a peak with his hands and mouth. He smiled, at the thought. He wanted Emily's eyes to be open so he could see them darken with desire when he touched her. His fantasy was just reaching the really interesting part when the subject of it burst into the room.

"Whitney, Your Grace, I need to speak with you. It is most important or I would not take you from your work."

"I was already somewhat distracted." He smiled, coming from behind the desk, taking her in his arms, and kissing her.

Without hesitation or even conscious thought, her arms snaked around his neck and at the slightest pressure from his lips, she opened her mouth.

As their tongues entwined, he drew her closer, moulding her body to his, wanting to feel the soft warmth of her. His lips left hers to trail kisses from her brow, along the sensitive shell of her ear, along her jaw, and down her throat. He smiled at the wildly beating pulse he felt there. His head dipped lower as he bent his head and kissed the crest of her breasts. His smile grew wider as he heard her sharp intake of breath.

Emily could only watch with widened eyes as his hands went to the fastenings of her bodice. "Your Grace, Whitney, Robert, what are you doing?"

His eyes gleamed as he released her breasts to his hungry gaze, his body tightened as he rubbed his thumbs lightly over their sensitive buds, causing them to harden. She sagged against him as her body became pliant.

"My Emily," he whispered as he bent his head. "I do not believe I shall ever stop wanting you."

Emily could not speak, could not form a comprehensible thought as his tongue swirled. She could barely breathe. She only knew she did not want him to stop. Then he did precisely that. She looked up at him in both surprise and regret as he deftly set her garments to rights.

"If I do not stop now, my love, I will not be able to stop. When we are married, I shall enjoy making love to you in every room in every house I own, but I intend to do the honourable thing and wait until we are married…even if it kills me," he added with a note of grim determination before kissing the tip of her nose and settling her on the sofa. He then perched a hip on the edge of the desk in an attempt to take his mind away from the pleasant prospect of Emily's *décolletage*.

"Now what did you come in here to talk to me about?" he said pleasantly.

Emily took a deep breath. "I came to talk to you about Lady Walmesly, Arabella."

Robert's mouth became a harsh line. "I do not wish to talk about Arabella either now or at any time in the future."

"But—" Emily began.

He held up a hand. "Arabella took the diamonds with the intention of making you take the blame. She must face the consequences of her crime," he said harshly.

"You cannot mean to report her to the authorities."

Emily was horrified. She was no friend of Arabella's but the thought of the girl's incarceration or transportation left her cold. Arabella would not survive nor would her parents survive the scandal. The whole family would be punished for one silly girl's foolish actions.

"I do not know what I shall do," Robert admitted. "I should have reported her already," he added, remembering the conversation he'd had with Burrows who had pointed out that had it been one of the servants he would not have hesitated to report the matter to the authorities.

"Could you not find some other way?" Emily asked.

Robert smiled at his tender hearted fiancée. "You are too kind to the girl."

"Arabella is a young and foolish girl. All her life she has been brought up to believe she had to make a brilliant marriage. To become a duchess was the only measure of her success. When she saw a threat to that ambition, she panicked and acted without thought. Surely you can find it in your heart to forgive her this one indiscretion," Emily pleaded.

"It was a crime," he persisted, but conceded that Emily's reasoning was sound.

"It was," she agreed. "I am not saying Lady Walmesly should go unpunished, but perhaps there is some other way to do so."

"Would not that suggest one law for the rich and another for the poor? Arabella gets off because she is wealthy with rich friends, but some poor fellow who steals a loaf of bread to feed his family is hauled off to prison."

"I believe the law should apply to all. No one should be above the law. However, I believe the man who steals to feed his family should be given work to do in the community, so should Arabella, who has done one stupid thing in a moment of madness, do something to make reparation for her crime."

"How do you propose to do that?" he asked with growing interest.

Emily considered for a moment before replying. "Perhaps the man could do something such as… work for the baker from whom he stole for a day a week for a number of months, or mend a roof, or something that made use of his skills and helped the community at the same time. Perhaps Arabella could start a school for the children of the poor, but spend time there, not just pay for it and walk away without another thought. Each time she attended she would be reminded of her crime and at the same time, some good would come from it."

"And how would this reflect justice? Should there not be some punishment?" he said.

"There are more ways of punishing than taking a person's liberty or life," she countered. "For example, the man who has to work for the baker may lose one day's pay each week, but at least he will still earn money on the other days."

"I don't see how this is sufficient punishment for the crime committed."

Emily gazed at him calmly. "When the man is in prison or transported, who is being punished?"

"Why, the thief of course."

"That is quite right," she agreed. "But when the man is punished, who is to earn money to feed his wife and children? Not only is he punished, but his family as well. Surely that is not right when they have done nothing wrong?"

"So you believe that if criminals are able to work off their penalties, this would be a fairer and better system?"

Emily frowned. "I don't know, but I think it may be better for some crimes, though we shall always need prisons for those whose crimes are violent and dangerous."

Robert looked at Emily with new respect. "You have given this much thought. I am getting a wife who is both beautiful and wise, not to say radical in her ideas. I rather think the ton will find you more than entertaining." He laughed. "Though I believe you might be as well to leave some of your more extreme views at home or they may think you are a French revolutionary."

Emily rolled her eyes. "You will consider what I said?"

"I will consider it."

"I am sure your brother will be most grateful."

"My brother? What has James to do with this?"

Emily laughed. How could a man be so obtuse? Then again, his mother had been equally unobservant. "Your brother is in love with Arabella." She rose, shaking her head as she left the room, leaving Robert with his mouth open.

Robert watched her go with a mixture of pride, amusement, longing, and respect. With every conversation, he loved her more. He was intrigued by her radical views on the penal system and, though he personally wanted to strangle Arabella, but not for stealing the diamonds. Somehow he had always believed Burrows would have turned them up somewhere. Had he not found Emily again, he could never have found it in his heart to forgive Arabella. He knew that and part of him still struggled with the thought that he should report her to the authorities, but he knew Arabella had quickly gotten out of her depth. When she had taken the jewels, she had never intended for things to get so out of hand and then she had panicked and tried to get rid of them. Could he ruin her life for a foolish mistake?

On the other hand, if what Emily had just said was true, could he bear to have Arabella as his sister-in-law?

Chapter Twenty-One

Emily stood before the cheval mirror, her brow furrowed in a frown. Earlier in the day boxes had arrived from Madame Chantelle's. She and Alice had giggled as they surveyed some of the gowns that had been ordered and blushed as they inspected the nightgowns and lingerie that had arrived. Emily had always considered corsets to be functional garments, but as she and Alice unpacked a dozen in a myriad of colours in silk and lace, she could not help but think it would be a shame only she and her maid would see them.

"I don't even remember ordering these," she exclaimed, holding up a corset that looked nothing like the sturdy ones she wore. Indeed, it seemed so small she wondered how it would fit.

Alice blushed to the roots of her hair. "I believe his grace sent a note to Madame Chantelle's to ask her to ensure nothing was missed, my lady."

Emily also blushed. How stupid of her to forget Robert no doubt had a great deal of knowledge of women's undergarments. She had experienced for herself how quickly he could both undo and re-do clothing. No doubt he had many years of practise. She gave herself a mental shake. It was not Robert's past that concerned her, but their future together. He had chosen her as his wife. She only hoped she could live up to his expectations.

She had made her bow privately at court. Like everything else, it was accomplished smoothly and quickly. She was only now beginning to realise the wealth and power of the family into which she was about to marry. Emily had to confess she was enjoying herself enormously and

Robert was enjoying showing off his bride-to-be. The mantelpiece overflowed with invitations to balls, the theatre, and musicales. It seemed everyone in London was curious to see who had landed the eligible Duke of Whitney.

The ton would have been very surprised to see the fiancée of the Duke of Whitney disappear down the backstairs of his magnificent town house every Thursday evening dressed in drab clothes, walk to the end of the street, hire a hansom, and travel to Cheapside. Whitney always spent Thursday at his club, and Lady Tremaine visited her friend Lady Cookham for cards. After three weeks of sitting on her own, Emily decided she would train the choir for the Advent service.

Her choir welcomed her as though she had been away for years. It had not been the same without her. She was a little uneasy, knowing Robert would not approve, but once he heard the choir sing, she felt he would forgive her for disobeying him. She was always careful to dress plainly and to slip in and out of Cheapside and Mayfair without anyone noticing, or so she thought.

Only three weeks remained until the Advent service. After that, she, Robert, and Lady Tremaine would travel down to Hampshire for the Solstice Ball and the wedding on Christmas Eve. Robert had suggested they have the wedding in London before the ton disappeared to their country estates for the festive season, but Emily had pleaded with him for a quiet wedding in the chapel at Charleton and had laughingly reminded him he would have no excuse for forgetting their anniversary if it was on Christmas Eve.

Her first real test would come at Lady Bainbridge's Ball, the highlight of the Little Season before everyone went to their estates for Christmas. The theatre visits and musicales had been small affairs. Lady Bainbridge's Ball would be the grandest affair she had attended. Everyone would be there, including, she had heard, some royalty. She was almost dressed when there was a knock at her bedroom door.

Lady Tremaine entered, already dressed in a gown of topaz with silver trimming and a matching turban. Even in her middle years Emily could see the great beauty she had once been.

The older woman smiled. "You look lovely my dear, you will be the talk of the ball tonight. I can see my son will have to take his place in the line of gallants who will want to dance with you."

Emily stood and looked at herself in the glass. Alice had worked her magic and tamed her chestnut curls so that they fell in a glossy sheet over her shoulder and had worked in a set of gold and emerald pins. The gown had been delivered earlier. It was cut lower than Emily liked and, in her opinion, revealed more décolleté than was proper, but it was too late to do anything about it now. The fabric was, she had to admit, the finest she had ever worn. The emerald green silk was shot through with the lightest gold thread. It shimmered with her slightest movement.

She smiled back at her future mother-in-law. "I hope his grace will approve."

"Robert is waiting in the green salon for you. He bid me to come and find you so that we may be off directly. You go down and I will bring your shawl."

When she entered the room, Robert was standing with his back to her, looking into the flames, a glass in his hand. He had not heard her enter and she was glad of a moment to collect her thoughts. Many women were considered beautiful, but Robert, in his black formal clothes was the epitome of male beauty. His height and broad shoulders would always mark him out in a room. His tightly cut jacket and breeches emphasised the muscled body beneath. The firelight highlighted the planes and shadows of his handsome profile.

As though he was aware of her thoughts, he turned and saw her. There was a moment of silence as they drank in each other.

"My God, Emily." He set his glass on the mantelpiece before striding to her and drawing her into his arms. He crushed her against him, his lips on hers urging a response.

Emily could not think, could barely breathe, every atom of her body responded to him. When he raised his lips, she could not help but sigh with regret.

"Soon, my little one, I shall not have to content myself with stopping at a kiss." He savoured the sweet scent of her hair.

Emily leaned against him. There was nowhere else she would ever want to be but in his arms.

His response was instant. "You don't know what you do to me," he muttered as he captured her lips again. This time they were both breathless. When they finally broke apart, Robert seated her on the sofa before resuming his place by the fireplace.

"You wanted to see me, Your Grace?" Emily began."

"Mmmm?"

"Your Grace asked me to see you before we go to the ball," she prompted, before laughing. "Your Grace, I think you will find it easier to concentrate if you look at my face."

Robert looked up and grinned. "You cannot blame a man for being distracted, though in future I think it best if you wear that gown when we are married and alone."

Emily rolled her eyes. "Your Grace, this is the latest fashion. It was you, Sir, who determined I should be dressed by Madame Chantelle."

"I must be insane," he muttered. "Madame Chantelle knew exactly what she was doing. No man will be able to tear his eyes away from your er…charms."

Emily laughed. "Is that what all this fuss is about? My goodness, if I had known I could have this effect, I should have bought a gown like this a long time ago. Perhaps then someone would have offered for me and I could have saved the estate years ago."

Robert took her hands, his eyes blazing into hers. "Don't even think it. Somehow, somewhere, someone determined you and I are meant to be together. You are the only woman I have ever or will ever love, Emily, and I think it is the same for you."

Emily regarded him solemnly. "You are right, my lord. When I was a young girl I dreamed of being rescued by a handsome knight in shining armour, and all the time I think I was waiting for you."

Robert bowed. "I am honoured to be your knight." He reached behind him and handed her a jewel box. Emily's glance shot from the box in her hand to his eyes. He smiled.

"Open it. I can assure you it does not contain a snake."

Obediently, Emily opened the jewel box and caught her breath. Against the black velvet lining nestled a magnificent suite of emeralds, each row contained exquisite teardrop emeralds which flashed and sparkled in the firelight.

Emily closed the lid with a snap. "Please, Your Grace, Robert, I cannot wear these."

Robert was amazed, he had never known a woman so reluctant to own and wear jewels. "Why not? They are my gift to you to mark our betrothal along with this." He slipped the diamond ring onto her hand. "I want everyone at the ball tonight to know that you are promised to me." He smiled. "But I don't understand your reluctance to wear the emeralds, the first of many jewels I intend to shower you with. I had them made for you because they reflect the colour of your eyes."

Emily took a breath before looking into his eyes. "I am honoured and proud to wear your betrothal ring," she began. "The emeralds are magnificent, they truly are. It's just that…" She hesitated. "It's just that last time I wore jewels everything went so wrong. I lost you and I thought I would never see you again, but worse than that, you thought I was a liar and a thief and I couldn't bear it."

Robert gathered her into his arms. "My darling, if I could turn back the clock, believe me I would. No one regrets more than I the time we spent apart and the vile things I said and did. I was a fool, an irrational, jealous fool. But we cannot allow the past to dominate our future. Please, wear the jewels, as a token of our new beginning. I love you so much, Emily, I cannot bear the thought of what my life would have been like without you. It would have been at best half a life."

He waited for her nod before he carefully fastened the necklace around her neck, kissing the sensitive hollow of her throat as he did so and then hanging the earrings in her ears. "When we are married I shall want to see you wearing only these in my bed," he whispered. A moment later, the bracelet was in place but not before Robert had rubbed his thumb over her wrist in lazy circles, creating a sensual haze from which Emily was not sure she wanted to emerge.

"I think we must go to the ball or Lady Bainbridge will think we are not coming. Though for two pins I would stay here and hang the ball," Robert muttered and Emily could see the passion in her own eyes reflected in his.

"That would not do at all Robert Tremaine," his mother announced from the door "For either of your reputations. Now come along. Emily, you look exquisite, and Robert try not to look as though you are about to devour Miss Conrad," she commanded as she led to way to the waiting carriage, smiling.

Chapter Twenty-Two

Bainbridge House was ablaze with candles at every window and huge braziers outside. A crush of carriages met them as guests arrived, shouting greetings to each other as they ascended the marble steps to the door. Liveried footmen lined the route from the carriage to the door and more took cloaks. The entrance hall was a huge marble and gilt room with two matching staircases curving up to the ballroom. The hundreds of candles became thousands as they reflected from the huge mirrors that adorned the walls. Yet more footmen mingled with the guests with trays of champagne.

"My goodness." Emily gazed at the crowd, awed by it all. "I have never seen so many beautiful women."

Robert smiled down at, her taking her arm. "You are the most beautiful. Come, my love, I think Lady Bainbridge will fall from the balcony if she leans over much farther. I had best introduce you."

He could not help but notice Emily was completely oblivious to the effect she had. All over the room people were turning to look at her as they made their way to their hosts. He caught odd snatches of conversations. Some of which made his smile widen.

"Of course, she's beautiful. Whitney always has beautiful women."

"Never thought he'd marry, but I can see why he's tempted."

"Heard she was a plain lass from the country. That can't be her."

"Heard she rides better than any man."

"Plays the pianoforte like an angel I heard."

"Have you seen the colour of her eyes, I'd never have believed eyes could be that shade of green if I hadn't seen them for myself."

Other comments caused his smile to slip.

"Heard his mother doesn't approve."

"Who is she? A nobody from the country with no connections or fortune. He'll be after another mistress within six months."

"I heard she was a chamber maid."

"She looks well enough, but jewels and a fine gown do not a lady make."

"Everyone thought he would marry the Walmesly girl, so I believe did she."

He hoped Emily had not heard the cruel and unkind comments but threw back his head with laughter when she turned to him and spoke. "It would seem the reviews are mixed so far, my lord."

He leaned down towards her. "You must remember, my dear, we are among some of the most critical, hypocritical, and hypercritical individuals on the face of the earth, and by criticising you they are hoping to draw attention away from their own faults and failures. Believe me, there are few occasions in London where wives and mistresses don't greet each other as friends."

Emily's eyes widened. "And does the one know about the other?"

"Sometimes they are friends, and in the case of the Earl of Darton, his wife, once she had done her duty and delivered him an heir and two spares, suggested he take his pleasure with Lady Wentworth, thus leaving her free to pursue her affair with Sir Richard Alton."

"Good gracious, I don't think I shall ever get used to the ton's way of doing things."

He placed his hand on hers and she felt the muscles in his arm flex. "You do not have to my love, for you will be both my wife and my mistress." He laughed as Emily blushed.

By the time they reached the receiving line, Emily had recovered her composure. As she rose from her curtsey, Lady Bainbridge embraced her warmly and commanded Robert to take good care of her. The Earl congratulated Robert on finding the most beautiful girl in London.

News of Robert's arrival with his fiancée had already reached the ballroom. There, every head turned as their names were announced. It seemed that the members of society who had not yet seen Emily wanted to do so now. Realising that the attention would be intense, Robert swept Emily onto the floor for a waltz.

"People are staring at me." Her smile wobbled. She knew marriage to Robert would entail a degree of public life, but it was only just dawning on her how much interest there would be.

"Impertinent chit," he teased. "I think you will find they are staring at me. Now concentrate and try not to stamp on my feet."

He pulled her closer and led her into a series of intricate turns and whirls so that she had to concentrate and forgot about the crowd who had now stopped what they were doing and watched the handsome couple dominate the floor. When the dance ended with a flourish, Emily dropped a deep curtsey to her handsome fiancé who drew her to her feet and planted a kiss on both of her gloved hands, to the applause of all in the room.

"Just as I thought," an elderly Marchioness observed. "Whitney has found his match, and it is definitely a love match."

"But who are her people? She seems to have no family connections," her equally elderly companion murmured.

"It really does not matter. From what I hear, in a few weeks she will be a member of one of the richest and most powerful families in the country. She will be the one whose connections are sought," replied the shrewd old lady.

"I heard," went on the third member of the group, "that she is the daughter of a poor knight, so she was brought up as a gentlewoman, though there is no money."

"Whitney has no need of money. He's as rich as Croesus," the Marchioness replied testily. "What he does need is an heir and, by the looks of it, there will be one before the end of their first year of marriage." She cackled as her companions nodded. Emily had passed the first test, the grande dames of the ton had accepted her.

At the end of the dance, Robert and Emily were surrounded by a crowd, most of them knew Robert but were keen to be introduced to his fiancée. Once Emily realised his friends were curious rather than critical, she began to enjoy herself. Robert soon found himself cast in the role of bystander as one after the other of his friends sought permission to dance with her.

He smiled to himself. At the Solstice Ball he had, he now recognised, been jealous of every man who had danced with her. Tonight he was happy to watch her on the dance floor, knowing these men would only hold her once. He would hold her and much more for the rest of their lives.

He sensed, rather than saw the figure come and stand beside him. "It's been a long time, brother," James said.

"I expected you to come with mother." Robert spoke to his brother, but his eyes never left Emily who was dancing with Lord Risely.

"Things were a little...ah...complicated," James admitted.

"How exactly?" Robert kept his tone carefully neutral.

James took a steadying breath, then replied, "What with the situation with Bella."

Robert finally turned, his blue eyes piercing his brother's. "Ah yes, how is Lady Walmesly?"

James grabbed two glasses of champagne from a passing servant, handed one to Robert and downed the other in one before continuing. "Bella is truly sorry for what she did, truly. She acted on a stupid, childish impulse and before she knew it, things had gotten totally out of hand. I cannot tell you how much she regrets her actions that night."

"Is she here tonight?"

"She hasn't been out of the house for months. She is afraid she will run into you or your mother and that you will cut her dead."

"She could suffer far worse than the cut direct."

James' face paled. "I know."

Robert's features hardened into a mask of contempt. "So she sent you to plead for her."

James shook his head. "No, she does not even know I am here. In fact, she expects the authorities any day and says it is no more than she deserves. I am here on my own behalf." Robert said nothing.

"I know Bella always set her cap at you, brother, and mother and her parents encouraged her, but the truth is, I love her, always have. I knew if you and she married, you would both be miserable. While I thought you were happy to go along with it, I bit my tongue and said nothing. When Miss Smith, er, Conrad came on the scene, I had hope. For the first time I saw you with a woman who did not appear to bore you. Bella saw it too and it made her desperate."

"So she stole the diamonds and almost convinced me Emily had stolen them. You do realise, brother, had the diamonds not turned up because Arabella tried to sell them, it could have been Emily dangling at the end of a rope?" Robert ground out.

"If she could wipe it out, she would, believe me, brother." James took a deep breath. "Bella is ill. She eats barely enough to keep body and soul alive. She hardly speaks and grows weaker by the day. It's my belief she is punishing herself for the great wrong she did. If she continues, I do not think she will live more than a few months."

Robert was shocked. Arabella Walmesly had always been so strong and determined. He struggled to picture her as James described. "I am sorry, of course, but there is nothing I can do for her."

"But there is," James replied quickly. "I believe if you and Miss Conrad were to see Bella so she could ask for your forgiveness, I think she might stand some chance of recovery."

"Out of the question. I will grant I shall not press any charges against her, but I have no wish to see Arabella Walmesly ever again, and neither will Emily." Both his face and his voice were implacable.

"Neither will Emily what?" Robert and James had not noticed the dance had ended and Emily was now at their side.

"James, how lovely to see you again." Emily stood on her toes and kissed his cheek. "We expected you weeks ago."

"James had pressing business as he has tonight. Good night, brother," Robert said firmly.

"Oh what a shame, I was looking forward to dancing with James, and I most certainly want to know what Emily will not do. Now we can either have the conversation here, Your Grace, or James will tell me when we are dancing." She smiled at her husband-to-be. "I would remind you, Sir, I have not taken any vow of obedience yet."

"And I fully expect the church to be struck by lightning when you do," he said wryly, nodding at James.

"It's Bella. I know she has done you a great wrong and so does she, but she is suffering, Miss Conrad. I believe that were you to see her so she can beg forgiveness, she might stand a chance of recovery."

Emily's face reflected her concern. "Poor Lady Walmesly. We must see her, Robert."

"I have already explained to my brother that, although I shall not be reporting Arabella to the authorities, I have no intention or desire to see her again," Robert said.

"And this is the thing that Emily will not do as well is it?" she demanded.

"It is." Robert's features appeared to be almost carved in granite.

"Sir, should we not be a little more charitable about this?" she said softly, threading her arm through his.

"I consider I have been charitable enough in not having her detained and tried for her crimes."

"Indeed you have, my love, and I am sure Lady Arabella and Lord James are more than grateful, but what harm would it do us to go and see her if it will do her some good."

Robert sighed. "I suppose when you put it like that I cannot refuse. Have Lady Walmesly call on us tomorrow."

The relief was etched on James' face. "I thank you from the bottom of my heart, Miss Conrad, but if I could prevail on your goodness a little further, Bella is not well enough to leave the house. Would it be possible for you to call on her?"

Chapter Twenty-Three

Robert had not said a word since they got into the carriage. His mouth was set in a grim line.

"I could quite easily go alone, if you would prefer," Emily said quietly.

He turned towards her. "I said I would accompany you and I shall. I find it difficult to contemplate seeing Arabella again when I think of the harm she has done you."

"Arabella did us both a great harm, but it is over now. We must not let the hurts of the past spoil our future."

Robert looked at his fiancée with a mixture of love and pride, "When did you become so wise?"

Emily's eyes twinkled. "Wisdom is a gift my lord. Some of us have it and some do not."

Robert grinned. "I suppose you are going to remind me of that fact at regular intervals."

"Every day of our marriage, so that you do not forget." She laughed happily.

The journey was not a long one, but there were many coaches and carts as travellers arrived in the city and tradesmen tried to deliver their goods. Emily was amused that Robert seemed to know who lived in most of the houses.

"That monstrosity belongs to the Duke of Horsham. It would appear he has as much taste in architecture as he has in women."

"How so?"

"Large and vulgar," Robert replied. Emily could not help but smile.

"That house belongs to Sir Richard de Courcey. If we are at a ball and he asks to dance with you, I strongly advise that you refuse?"

"But why? Does he have such a bad reputation?"

"Indeed he does...." He paused.

"I assume that having brought it up, you are going to tell me what it is."

"He is the biggest gossip in London. Anything you say will be in the newspaper the next day."

"Oh for heaven's sake, I thought you were going to tell me something really exciting." Emily rolled her eyes.

"And he is an inveterate lecher, so I don't want to see you within fifty yards of him," he said firmly.

"And to whom does this house belong?" She pointed towards an elegant mansion with white marble pillars.

"That is the house we are visiting. Walmesly had the old house knocked down and this built."

"In the expectation his daughter would be marrying a duke?"

"Perhaps so."

Further conversation was impossible as the carriage pulled to a halt and they disembarked.

The earl came down the steps to meet them. "Good of you to come, Whitney, Miss Conrad." He paused to wipe his face with a handkerchief. "Can't tell you how sorry I am about this whole business."

He led the way through the marble hall and into the salon where James and the countess were standing. The worry of the last few weeks had clearly taken their toll on both the earl and the countess. Gone was the easy confidence they had when Emily first met them at Charleton.

The countess curtseyed deeply to Robert. "Thank you, Your Grace." Her lips trembled.

"Your thanks are misplaced, madam, and should go to my fiancée. She persuaded me there might be an alternative way of dealing with the situation." His words were stern but his voice was gentle.

"Lady Walmesly, perhaps I could see Lady Arabella now," Emily suggested quietly.

"Of course, Miss Conrad. Bella is in her sitting room."

"I'll escort you," James offered.

At the door, James paused. "Whitney, I must have your promise that you will keep your temper. Bella is fragile, very fragile indeed, and I am concerned that it will take only the smallest thing to tip her over the edge."

Before Robert could form a reply Emily spoke. "Would it be better if I were to see Lady Arabella alone at first, so she doesn't feel intimidated?"

"I think it would," James replied with a look of relief.

Robert opened his mouth to object, but caught the look in Emily's eyes and sighed. "I suppose you're right. Do you think Walmesly has anything decent to drink?"

James nodded. "It's the one thing for which he's known. He boasts he has the best cellar in London."

"Then let us see if he is right. Emily, I will be back in half an hour."

* * * *

Bella's sitting room was semi-dark The blinds were drawn and it took Emily a moment for her eyes to adjust to the light. A slight movement drew her attention to the sofa. Arabella was lying there. Emily could scarcely control her shock. Instead of the ethereal beauty she remembered, Arabella seemed to have shrunk. Her hair had lost its lustre and hung in lifeless strands. She had clearly lost weight. Her gown hung loosely from her shoulders and her skin was pale and drawn, making her eyes appear huge and her lips almost colourless.

"Miss Conrad," the ghostly figure whispered, as though the life had left her voice as well. "It is so good of you to come. I know I do not deserve your forgiveness."

"Oh Lady Arabella, what has happened to you?"

"I am being punished, Miss Conrad. God is punishing me for my wickedness, and it is nothing less than I deserve."

Emily came and sat beside her erstwhile rival. "I do not think it is God who is punishing you, Lady Arabella. I think you are punishing yourself."

The huge blue eyes surveyed her. "Either way, I am being punished and deservedly so. I have ruined my family. I pushed my father to the brink of ruin, demanding he build this house and re-model the castle. There is little money left, and I did it for vanity, thinking I should become

126

a duchess, a leader of society. I thought it was my right to marry Whitney. All my life I have been given what I wanted."

"Lady Arabella, you do not need to speak of this," Emily began.

"Forgive me, Miss Conrad, but there is every need, especially to you whom I have wronged most. I need to tell you, so that at the end, even if you cannot find it in your heart to forgive me, you will at least understand." Emily nodded, sensing that the other woman needed to unburden herself.

"I have had plenty of time to consider this," she continued. "My mother and father were not a love match. Their marriage was arranged by their fathers. Even as a child I knew there was little love between them, though they both showed love to me. When my brother died, it became obvious there would be no heir. Mother could not have more children. So, all the hopes and expectations began to rest on me.

"I was to make a brilliant marriage not only to restore the family's social position, but also its fortunes. Papa was not, is not a great manager of his estates and had made some investments that failed. Of course, none of this was known. When one has a title, it is possible to maintain the air of success long after it has gone.

"As you know, my mother and Whitney's mother have been friends since they were in the schoolroom. So, because they were friends, my mother pushed for me to be considered a suitable bride for Whitney. Somehow she persuaded Lady Tremaine and I was dispatched to ensure Lady Tremaine approved of me, which she did. The only two things mama failed to take into consideration were Whitney's feelings on the matter and you, Miss Conrad." Arabella paused.

"Had you not fallen at his feet, literally as it happens, Mama's grand plan might have worked. Whitney had inherited and knew the importance of marrying and producing legitimate heirs. At the time I don't think he particularly cared whom he married. Once the succession was secure, he would have gone his way and I would have gone mine." She paused again, regarding Emily thoughtfully. "Does this shock you, Miss Conrad?"

Emily thought of the few memories she had of her own parents. "No, it doesn't shock me. I just find it sad. Couples promise to love and cherish each other, yet there does not seem to be much room for that in this kind of arrangement."

"The romantic notion of love and marriage is increasingly irrelevant the higher up one moves in the social scale," Arabella affirmed.

"Then it would seem better to have been born a farmer's daughter. At least they have the chance to marry for affection," Emily countered.

Lady Arabella smiled briefly, and for a moment Emily could see the beauty she had been. "I think you are right. That is why society women put so much effort into being grand hostesses and doing charitable works. They have to find an outlet for their personalities if their husbands do not care. I believe it also enables them to look in the glass with some pride when their husbands take a mistress. There are, of course, the wives who console themselves with gowns and jewels. If their husband is going to stray, they make him pay, There are some ton marriages that end in love even if they did not begin with it. I had hoped Whitney and I would be one of those." She stopped, lost in thought for a moment of what might have been.

"Then Robert rescued you, Miss Conrad, and things changed," she continued. "I knew almost from the first time I met you that all Mama's plans were for naught. Whitney could not take his eyes off you. Now I have to tell you, Miss Conrad, that I am grateful to you."

Emily had not expected hear that, "How so?"

The other woman smiled again. "I am grateful to you now, but as you can imagine, at the time I thought my life was over. Everything I had hoped for and planned for had been taken away from me by someone I considered to be my inferior. I hope I do not upset you, Miss Conrad, but I have learned the painful way that honesty is best in the long run."

Emily nodded. "I am not offended."

"At first I thought Whitney would, after the novelty of meeting you had worn off, remember his obligations, especially as Lady Tremaine so approved of our match. To be fair, Whitney had never offered, nor had he ever indicated he intended to." She smiled ruefully. "I just could not believe he was not falling in with my plans. That he was not… falling in love with me." She closed her eyes.

"Lady Arabella, if this is exhausting you, I can go away and come back another time," Emily said quietly.

"No, Miss Conrad, I must finish this. You have been more than kind in coming here after all I have done to you."

Emily saw tears shimmering in her eyes. "Please, Lady Arabella, you must not upset yourself."

The other woman looked at her in admiration. "Even now, you behave with the grace and dignity of a duchess. Whitney has chosen well." She paused for a moment.

"The night of the Solstice Ball I honestly do not know what possessed me. Whitney told me he was going to marry you, and I was overtaken by what I can only describe as a kind of madness. When you said you were going away, I knew I had to discredit you. Without that I knew Whitney would not rest until he found you.

"When you gave me the note and the diamonds, you handed me the perfect weapon. It was as though I was another person. Once I told Whitney, I realised I had done something terribly wrong. Oh Miss Conrad, I cannot tell you how much I regret my actions, yet I did not know what to do. Instead of confessing, I kept quiet and compounded my crime by trying to sell the diamonds. I foolishly thought if I got rid of them, the problem would go away."

Lady Arabella lapsed into silence before she continued. "I know I have no right to hope for your forgiveness, and I do not blame you. James told me of the situation in which you were living until you were restored to Robert. It is important for you to know I sincerely regret everything I have done and will spend the rest of my life trying to make amends." She wept quiet tears.

Without a second thought, Emily gathered the sobbing woman into her arms. Lady Arabella Walmesly was no longer the haughty society beauty, but a shadow. Her looks and fortune were gone. Everything she had been brought up to believe about herself and her place in the world was gone. Even though Arabella had caused Emily much pain, she could not feel hatred or anger towards her. All she could feel was pity.

Chapter Twenty-Four

"Are you going to tell me where we are going, my lord?" Emily said.

"I told you, my love, it's a surprise." Robert's hand guided her as she edged gingerly forwards. He had insisted on a blindfold, telling her the surprise would be worth it. As he blindfolded her he could not resist kissing her behind her ear and promising himself that one day he would have Emily blindfolded and naked in his bed.

"You can open your eyes now."

Emily stood for a moment letting her eyes adjust to the light. They were in a small courtyard when suddenly the door to the stable opened. Emily's breath caught in her throat.

"Apollo? Is it really Apollo?" she murmured as she walked slowly towards the horse. As she stroked its nose, the horse nuzzled her hand. "Oh Apollo, I have missed you." She turned to Robert. "I will never be able to thank you enough, Your Grace. How did you find him?"

Robert returned her smile. "I went to the livery where you sold him when you came to London. He is such a magnificent horse it was not difficult to track him down. In the end, it turned out that he was being treated very well by an old friend of mine. After I explained Apollo was so important to my bride, he was only too pleased to sell him back to me." At twice the price he bought him for, Robert added silently, but he realised nothing gave him more pleasure than giving pleasure to Emily.

"Come on, my lady. We need to be off. Apollo needs the exercise, and we both need a break from London society."

Within minutes, they were both mounted and riding out. Emily relaxed. Robert was right; the rules of society were exhausting. Every time she went out she was concerned she would make a terrible cake of herself, but as always her husband-to-be was there, leading, guiding, and supporting. She smiled at him, thanking her lucky stars their paths had crossed. She could not imagine her life without him. If she ever doubted his love, the fact that he had tracked down her horse told her all.

Robert caught the smile. "What?"

"I love you, Robert, with all my heart." she said simply.

Robert could not help himself. So few called him by his given name and he loved to hear it on Emily's lips. He grinned back at her.

"Then follow me, my lady, we have many miles to cover." He only had to give his stallion the slightest touch with his heels and they were off.

With the wind whistling through her ears, Emily could not have been happier. The streets of London fell away as they rode. Robert was always just a little way in front, but looking back to ensure she was keeping up with him.

After a few miles they stopped at the village of Wickham to rest the horses. The early mist had cleared, and it was a perfect, crisp autumn day, although weak the sun shone in a cloudless blue sky. The rolling hills gave them a perfect view. They could still see London in the distance, but they felt a million miles away from its rules of etiquette where the slightest infringement could mean social death. Here there were just the two of them; no one on their journey knew who they were, nor did they care. For the first time in weeks, they could just be themselves.

As Robert sat on a fallen log, Emily nestled at his side, his arm around her waist. He sighed in contentment and dropped a kiss on her head.

"Why the sigh, Your Grace?"

He looked down at her for a moment, wanting to memorise every detail. Emily looked particularly beautiful. The exercise had made her eyes sparkle and her cheeks rosy. The russet riding habit clung to her figure, emphasising her narrow waist and the ripe fullness of her breasts. The jaunty little hat lay abandoned on the grass.

"Oh so it's back to Your Grace now is it?" he teased. "I'll tell you what, my love, if you call me by my given name, you shall have a prize."

"A prize?" Emily repeated in mock amazement. "It must be a very valuable prize, Your Grace, to tempt a young lady to break one of the social rules that is more or less written in stone."

"This prize will not disappoint," he assured her.

Emily began to look theatrically around. "I'm not too sure, my lord. I don't see a sack of gold or diamonds, nor do I see a modiste with an armful of gowns, to say nothing of furs."

Robert was laughing as he drew her onto his lap. "The prize is rarer and more valuable than any of those baubles."

Emily arched an eyebrow. "Really, my lord? What could it possibly be?" She paused, running her tongue over her lips. "Robert?"

"This." His mouth captured hers, his tongue brushing her lips in a silent command; she opened her mouth wanting him to deepen the kiss. Her arms locked around his neck. The chaste and courtly kisses they'd shared as a betrothed couple in London were nothing like this. Emily was breathless yet she did not want the sensations to stop. She wanted to feel Robert's hands on her. She wanted to feel his naked skin against hers. Slightly shocked by her thoughts, she hesitated.

Robert was instantly aware. He was attuned to her in a way he had never been with any other woman, nor had he ever wanted to be. "What's the matter, sweet?" he whispered, his lips brushing a kiss against her ear and being rewarded as she shivered against him.

"When you kiss me, I think I am going to either explode or melt. Is this normal?"

Robert laughed, "It's beyond normal, my love. When we are married, I fully intend to make sure that you explode and melt from pleasure. In fact, it will be my husbandly duty to ensure it happens every night."

"That is a lot of kissing."

"There will be a great deal of kissing and a lot more besides." He took her hand in his as a thought occurred to him. "Emily, are you looking forward to our marriage?"

She looked at him in surprise. "Of course. How could you think otherwise?"

He returned her gaze steadily. "You know there are things that a man and wife do—in the marriage bed."

"I think so. I know there is something that happens in the marriage bed. It was something Sir Richard Cropton seemed to be keen on."

Robert's mouth thinned into a line. "What Cropton wanted to do to you was nothing like what will happen between us. If I ever lay my hands on that evil, twisted bastard, I will kill him."

Emily cradled his face in her hands. "I think Sir Richard is already being punished for his wickedness. He has no family and no money. He is more deserving of our pity than our anger."

Robert relaxed against her fingers. "You are more forgiving than I, my love. Though he is still a snake in the grass, I would not be at all surprised that having failed to secure your fortune, he has not sniffed out another poor female upon whom to prey."

"Let us forget about the odious Sir Richard. You were talking about the marriage bed."

Robert took a deep breath. This was not a conversation he had expected to have, but he wanted Emily to approach their marriage as an equal. A part of him had always thought the reason so many ton marriages were unhappy was because the brides had no idea what to expect and their husbands were either over eager young men or marrying for duty. Neither of which provided a sound basis for developing a happy marriage.

"When we are married, we shall share the same bed."

"And there will be kissing," Emily interrupted.

"There will be kissing, and we shall hold each other and touch each other."

"I like the sound of that," she said boldly.

Robert inhaled sharply. From her response to him, he already knew his future wife had a passionate nature, though she did not know it. He looked forward to initiating her into making love.

"When we have kissed and touched, our bodies will join together."

Emily looked puzzled. "But how shall I know where to touch you, and how will our bodies join together?"

Robert looked up as though hoping for some divine help. None was forthcoming. He took another deep breath. "We shall have to experiment with the touching, but the general rule is that it should be pleasurable."

"Are you blushing, Your Grace?"

He could swear she was trying not to laugh. "Most certainly not. The sun is unseasonably warm, that's all."

"I still don't understand about the joining together business."

He was beginning to wish he had not started this conversation, but start it he had and he intended to finish it. "Emily, are you aware that men's bodies and women's bodies are different?"

"Yes," she replied warily.

"There is a part of a man that when the time comes, will fit inside a woman. Sometimes a child will be the result of this. Apart from the first time when there is some pain, it will be a pleasurable experience."

Emily shook her head. "It all seems terribly complicated."

He smiled. "I do not think I have explained it well, but when the time comes I will do something better. I'll show you."

He drew her to her feet. "Now let's be off. The horses are rested. Any more of this talk and we shall not get to where we are going."

As they rode on, Emily thought of the things Robert had said. It seemed a shame that there should be pain when the kissing and touching were so pleasurable. Truth to tell, she still was not entirely sure of how a man and a woman's body could fit together, but she had to admit, she liked the sound of it.

Chapter Twenty-Five

They rode in silence for a few miles, before Robert spoke again. "We turn in here."

They entered a tree lined avenue where leaves formed a carpet of red and gold beneath the horses' hooves. They left the main drive and walked the horses into the woodland. Eventually the path opened out and Emily's breath caught in her throat. There was a still lake, the trees perfectly reflected on its clear surface. Her eyes were drawn to a house at the far end with a small jetty in front to which were tied two rowing boats.

"What is this place?" she said in wonder.

"Our little piece of heaven," Robert replied. "Come, let's go to the house. I'm starved."

As they approached the building, Emily paused. "I have never seen a building quite like this."

"It is similar to some I have seen in Austria. I thought it would fit well by the lake. The steep pitch on the roof is good both for draining the rain and clearing the snow. Come inside."

It was bigger than Emily had first thought, and they were clearly expected because a cheerful fire blazed in the grate. The large windows let in the late Autumn sun and the sofas and chairs looked comfortable after their long ride. The dining table had been laid with bread, cheese, chicken, and fruit and a bottle of claret stood open. Robert enjoyed watching Emily's reaction to everything she saw.

"Whose house is this?"

"Ours," he replied. "Much of our life, whether we want it or not will be lived in public. We have great privileges, but we will also have responsibilities." He took her hand and kissed her fingers. "I want us to have a place, just for us so when life in London becomes too fraught and we don't have time to get down to Charleton, we can come here and escape for a little while at least."

His thoughtfulness brought tears to her eyes. "I wonder," she whispered, "what good deeds I must have done to have been rewarded with you for a husband?"

His fingers grazed her cheek. "It is I who is the fortunate one, my love, and I thank God I found you." He drew her into his arms and captured her lips, teasing her until she opened to him, her arms snaking around his neck.

When he stepped back, he whispered, "I don't think I shall ever get enough of you, Emily. I am beginning to wish we had married the day you came back to me."

She laughed happily. "We have a whole lifetime ahead of us, my lord."

"I don't think one lifetime will be enough," he muttered, dipping his head again.

Emily's laugh stilled in her throat. Once again she wanted him to strip her jacket and blouse away so she could feel his touch. The tension began to build as he deepened the kiss. It became almost unbearable when he broke the contact with her and stepped back.

"Come, my love. Much more of this and we will both reach the point of no return."

"Perhaps I already have," she said almost breathless.

He looked into her passion glazed eyes. He could take her there and then. She wanted him as much as he wanted her and God did he want her, body and soul. He wanted to bury himself in her so she would be his and his alone. He had never felt like this about any woman. Those he had bedded had been pleasant enough and he had always enjoyed them, but once the chase was over, they had both walked away without rancour or regret.

With Emily it was different. He could never walk away from her. He wanted her close to him for the rest of his life. He wanted to see her grow big with his babies and would still want her when there were silver hairs among the brown.

He sighed. "For once in my life I am going to take the noble path. Come, let's eat. I'm starved."

Emily had rarely enjoyed a meal more. Once she sat down, she realised she too was hungry. Robert entertained her with tales of his exploits as a soldier.

"You make me realise what a sheltered life I have led," she responded as he told her of the snow-capped Alps and the way the locals strapped narrow planks of wood to their feet to travel in the mountains.

"Then for our honeymoon, we shall travel to Europe," he declared, "before war breaks out again."

"Is war inevitable?"

"It is when there are hotheads who believe it to be so." He grimaced. "Foolish young men who have not yet learned the value of peace and family are one element and even more foolish old men who are willing to sacrifice the young ones for what? Often it's a patch of land with no use to anyone anyway. The fact is, when all is said and done, the politicians will have to get around a table and talk to settle matters. So why not put more effort into the talking at the beginning of the process?"

"Then you must ensure you take your place in society and advise those who take the decisions," she said firmly. "I don't doubt you need some project with which to occupy yourself. What better one could there be?"

"It is a huge undertaking and would mean much of our time would be spent in London."

"Then so be it. How foresighted of you to buy this place." She raised her glass.

"I will never be able to put into words the love I feel for you," he said, touching his glass to hers. "Now, I think we have time for a quick trip on the lake before we must head back."

"Certainly, Sir. Shall we make a wager?"

"You intend to row?" He could not hide his surprise.

"I most certainly do. Now I suggest we row once around the island and back to the jetty."

There was of course no question that Robert would not win, but he had to admit Emily gave him a fine race. They were neck and neck as they rounded the island, but he pulled ahead as they approached the pier.

Laughing, Emily took his hand as she stepped from the boat. "It was only the fact that women's clothing is so restrictive that you won."

He had removed his jacket and neck cloth and raced in his white shirt and buckskin trousers, the sight of which made her breathless.

"Nonsense, I won because I was the superior rower."

"Well I should like to see you do it in corsets and petticoats," she retorted.

"And I should like to see you do it without," he shot back.

She paused with her hands on her hips as a thought occurred to her. "When we make love, will I be naked?"

His head reared back in surprise. "We shall both be naked," he replied, wondering why on earth well brought up young ladies were kept in such ignorance.

"I see," she murmured, concerned that no-one had seen her naked. "Do we have to be…naked?

"We don't have to be but it will be better if we are," was his honest reply.

"So, to summarise,"—she counted on her fingers—"there will be nakedness, kissing, and touching, then we fit together."

He could barely keep a straight face. "That's about it, though it is much more exciting in the doing than the listing."

She shot him a hard look. "I am just trying to learn and understand, Your Grace."

He drew her once again into his arms and kissed her. His fingers tangled in her hair before he brushed them across the top of her breasts and then dipped them inside her bodice to brush the sensitive buds. He pulled her closer so that she could feel the hardness that seemed to be his permanent state whenever she was near.

There was nothing he wanted more than to take her to the soft bed he knew was already made up in the cabin's bedroom. To slowly strip her of her clothes and even more slowly caress her with his hands and tongue until she was writhing in sweet agony beneath him. Then he would slowly enter her and bring her to a stunning climax. He wanted to hear her call his name, but he would not do it now.

He stepped back. "Emily, believe me when I say there is nothing I want more than to make love to you right now, but I will not. I will not dishonour you or myself by taking your virginity before we are wed. If by some horrible trick of fate, I were killed before the wedding, you would be dishonoured and considered damaged goods by society. Your chances of finding a husband would be nil. You would be ruined so I cannot, will not, compromise you by giving in to the lust I feel. But, when we are married," he added leering outrageously, "I fully intend to give in to lust on every possible occasion."

Emily laughed in spite of herself. "Thank you, Robert." For the first time in her adult life she felt not only loved, but cherished.

Chapter Twenty-Six

The weeks passed. The mists and fogs of autumn gave way to the colder, crisper days of early winter. The 'little season' was in full swing. When she had time, Emily spent hours with Arabella. At first she had just sat with her, reading to her as Arabella listened quietly. For many weeks, Emily was concerned Arabella was not making any progress. She was often tearful and refused to see anyone other than her parents, Emily, and James.

One afternoon, Emily rose from the sofa and opened the drapes, letting the weak sunlight fill the room.

"What are you doing?" Arabella said. "I don't want the curtains open. I don't want to see outside."

"Arabella, you say you are sorry for what you have done, so it's time to do something about it," Emily said crisply.

Pale blue eyes focused on her. "I don't understand."

Emily took a deep breath, knowing what she said next would have a huge effect on Arabella. "Lady Arabella, I know you regret what you did and feel guilty but you cannot live the rest of your life shut away like this. You are young and made a foolish mistake. It's time to stop feeling sorry for yourself and think about other people."

The pale blue eyes opened wider. "You think I am being selfish?"

Emily smiled. "No, of course not, but skulking in a darkened room and cutting yourself off from the world is not the way to recover. You could do so much good with your life, but it won't happen if you lie here like one of the heroines in one of those ghastly novels you insist I read to you."

"But what can I do? I have been brought up to be a decorative wife. I have no skills of any practical use at all."

Emily took a deep breath. "You could teach."

"What? Become a governess? I assure you, Emily, my own experience with governesses was enough. I know I was not the brightest of pupils, but they seemed incapable of teaching me anything other than to be neat and tidy, to speak a little French, and read and write."

Emily smiled. "My plans are a little more ambitious than that." She went on to explain her own dealings with the people in Cheapside and the great need there. "If someone were to open a school, the children would be able to learn to read and write. It would give them an opportunity to earn more. There is a building near to the church. We could go out tomorrow and I could show you—"

"But what could I do?" Arabella interrupted. "I haven't the slightest idea how to teach."

Emily's smile grew wider. Arabella had not rejected the idea and, instead expressed interest. "You will be the one to raise the money to make it all happen. The building will require some repairs and, of course, the owner will have to be persuaded to rent it to us. Then there will be slates and chalks, primers, pens and ink to buy."

Arabella shook her head, "I would love to help, truly I would, but that would mean—"

"Going out into society again?" Emily finished. Arabella nodded.

Emily rose. "Then let us start now." She strode over to the fireplace and pulled the cord. "We shall start with a little fresh air in the garden, and, if that is not too taxing, we shall walk to the end of the street. You have to start somewhere." She held her breath, waiting for Arabella to refuse, but to her delight, the other woman stood.

Within minutes, the two women were wrapped in bonnets and shawls and strolling around the garden. The trees had shed their leaves and few plants had survived the first sharp frosts, but it did not matter. At the gate they paused.

Arabella hesitated. "I think I could manage a walk around the square."

Emily took her arm and they strolled together. As they wandered through the square, Emily insisted Arabella sit and rest for a few minutes.

Arabella turned to her. "I feel as though I have been living in a long dark tunnel, but I begin to see some light at the end of it. I will come with you tomorrow. I want to start the school."

Emily squeezed her arm. "I am so glad." She frowned slightly. "There is just one thing, I cannot come in Robert's carriage. I shall come in a hansom and you must wear your dowdiest clothes. Few people in Cheapside know my circumstances and I should like to keep it that way."

Arabella laughed. "Does Whitney by any chance know of your clandestine visits?"

Emily shook her head. "Not exactly. He knew I organised a choir when I lived there, but he does not know that I still do."

"And did he forbid you to continue?"

Emily nodded. "The Advent service is on Sunday. Beyond that I shall not continue, but I made a promise to the choir and I want to see it through."

"Don't worry, your secret is safe with me." Arabella grinned. "As we are to be partners in crime, I should like it if you would call me Bella." She laughed again. "I cannot wait to see Whitney's face when he sees your choir."

"Oh, he'll never know," Emily said airily. "I shall plead a headache and go to bed when Robert and Lady Tremaine go to church on Sunday, then go to the service, and be back in my bed before anyone knows I'm gone."

They were approaching Bella's house when a familiar voice hailed them. "Bella, is that you, and Miss Conrad?" James Tremaine was sitting in his barouche. "Could I tempt you two young ladies for a short drive?"

Emily looked at the other woman. "Perhaps you might call tomorrow. I think Bella needs to rest now, but we were about to take some tea, perhaps you could be persuaded to join us?"

James did not take much persuasion and Emily found herself cast in the role of chaperone while James and Bella chatted quietly, but she was pleased to see the fresh air had put some bloom back into Bella's cheeks and for the first time in many weeks, her conversation was animated.

"I cannot begin to thank you," James said as he expertly turned the corner back into Bruton Street. "Your visits to Bella have saved her life I am sure."

"That is kind of you, James, but I have only acted as any friend would."

"But Bella was not your friend, Emily. A lesser woman would have walked away from her and left her to rot. I begin to feel she will recover and the idea of the school you have suggested has fired her. She now feels there is a purpose to her life."

Emily laughed as he handed her from the carriage. "Once she gets her confidence back, I am sure she will enjoy the challenge. Now, come in, I'm sure Robert will want to know about this fine new vehicle."

Chapter Twenty-Seven

The church was packed for the Advent service. It seemed each member of the choir was related to half of the people in the east end. Ragged boys, mudlarks, and crossing sweepers sat on the floor at the front. The hum of chatter ceased as the organist played the introduction to the first carol of Advent.

Emily could barely breathe, in a few moments the choir, her choir, would sing. They sat at the front of the church, enjoying the music and enjoying still more the thought of the supper they had been promised at the end of the service. Feathers nodded on bonnets as the wives of market porters and costermongers greeted each other. Farther back clerks and some young lawyers sat with their wives and at the very back of the church the clothing got more colourful as the friends of the choir wore their finest clothes.

In the gated pews at the very back, some of the ton sat, the up and coming vicar had alerted some of his friends to the ragged choir led by a woman and their curiosity had been piqued. Arabella, James, and Robert were among them. The vicar's eldest brother had been at school with James who mentioned it to Robert who knew at once who the mystery female was.

He was furious. He had made it clear when he had brought Emily back from Cheapside that she was not to continue with this scheme. He was angry with her for secretly disregarding his wishes but more furious with her for putting her safety at risk. His first instinct was to lock Emily in her room, but he knew that would have no impact whatsoever. Instead, he had come along with James and Arabella to ensure Emily was safe. Whether she would be safe when he got her home would be an entirely different matter.

Near the door, Robert noticed a soberly dressed man observing the proceedings with avid interest. He turned to another man close to the door and with a slight shake of the head, the other man left. He was about to comment to his brother when the organ swelled, the service began and Robert's attention focused on Emily.

* * * *

Emily saw little of this. Her hands shook as she opened her music. At her signal, the choir stood as one. By the third bar she began to relax. Their voices blended together. The sopranos soared while the bass underpinned the harmony. After the chaotic rabble of their earlier rehearsals, they worked as one.

At the end of their performance a moment of silence followed before the church erupted with loud applause, much to Emily's amazement. She had expected a dignified quiet as the appropriate response in a church, but from the urchins at the front to the porters, chimney sweeps, costermongers and their wives, there was an exuberant response. Emily breathed a sigh of relief along with the vicar.

The rest of the service passed in a blur. Emily was glad when it ended. The stress of sneaking out to rehearse and keeping the secret from Robert had been a strain, although a part of her would have liked him to have seen what she had achieved.

The congregation had long since departed when she left the church. The bishop had detained her to talk about her interesting experiment with music. He had never heard a blend of both male and female voices before and enjoyed the novelty. He was impressed by the innovative ideas of the young vicar. Emily smiled to herself. It had not occurred to the bishop for one moment that innovative ideas could have come from a woman.

As she crossed the alley, a tall figure stepped out and grabbed her by the wrist. "I think you and I need to have a serious talk," a familiar voice said. "Now that you're to be a high and mighty duchess, I want my share of your inheritance. So see to it that it's done proper and above board, soon. If not, the next time I won't be so gentle. I want the money in my bank a week before you marry or your husband will be a widower on his wedding day."

Emily stumbled as her uncle abruptly released her and strode off into the enveloping darkness.

She was still staring after him when a carriage stopped beside her. The door opened and Robert stepped out, his face like thunder. "Who was that?" he demanded, nodding in the direction her uncle had taken.

"No one." She tried to bring her voice under control. "Just some-one wanting directions."

They travelled in silence, the tension almost unbearable by the time the carriage stopped. "I will give you ten minutes to freshen up and then I want to see you in my study," Robert growled as he handed her down. "My patience is stretched as far as it will go so do not keep me waiting."

Now that she was safely indoors, Emily's fear receded and anger began to take over. She would not go down to his study like a naughty child summoned by the headmistress. If he wanted to discuss the evening, they would do it in a civilised manner when Robert had calmed down and was willing to listen to reason. She sent Alice down fifteen minutes later with a message that she had a headache and would speak to him in the morning.

Less than two minutes later, the door to her room crashed open. "Out," he ordered Alice as he entered, locking the door behind the maid and pocketing the key.

"Robert, what do you think you're doing?" Emily sat in her nightrail, her hairbrush poised.

"What do I think I'm doing?" he said silkily. "I think I'm about to make it clear to my future wife that when I give her an order it is to be obeyed."

Emily stood up to face him. "Just how do you propose to do that? Beat it into me?"

She was unaware of the light catching her nightrail, making it almost transparent. Robert's breath caught in his throat as he drank in the sight of her from her pert breasts, the nipples peaked against the fabric, her narrow waist and long, shapely legs, a dark shadow between her legs hinting at the pleasure he might find there.

"It seemed a likely option when I left the study," he acknowledged, his own body responding to hers.

They stood in silence for several minutes.

"I forbade you to return to Cheapside," he said at last, his voice softening. "Not because I did not want you to pursue your wish, but because I was worried some harm could come to you."

She took a step towards him. "The people of Cheapside have been kind to me. When I was there on my own, they took me in and treated me like one of them. They would have kept me safe."

"If they had been there. You were on your own last night. Had that man been set upon harming you, no one was there to protect you. He could have abducted you or worse and no one would have known a thing about it until it was too late."

"But he did not," she replied evenly.

She could not betray her uncle, despite the vile things he had threatened. He was still her only living relative. Once she was married, she would meet with him and offer him half of her fortune. She was certain he would be reasonable.

"You still disobeyed me."

"I have not yet promised to do so," she observed.

"But you will. I will not have my wife cavorting about London and putting her life in danger."

"Cavorting?" She laughed. "I hardly think leading a choir in a church counts as cavorting."

He did not return her laugh. "I will not be swayed in this Emily. You will not compromise your safety or your reputation."

Her laughter ceased. "Now you are being ridiculous. How could my going to Cheapside possibly compromise my reputation?"

"Unmarried women are not supposed to be out unaccompanied. You know the rules. A reputation takes far more effort to regain than it does to lose it. If it can be regained at all." He sighed.

"I cannot believe you care a fig for reputation," she shot back. "I am beginning to think whoever is responsible for these ridiculous rules has the sole objective of making women's lives small.

He raised his eyebrows. "How so? Women are the weaker sex. These rules are put there to protect them."

"Physically, women may be the weaker sex. That I must accept, but social etiquette, as far as I can see, seems to be designed so women remain weaker in every sense of the term," she shot back.

"What evidence do you have to support such a statement?" His anger had dissipated and he was beginning to enjoy their verbal duel.

"The ridiculous waste of time spent changing into different dresses during the day, not to mention what you do not see of the garments underneath which must be designed to punish women for some previous sin."

"And what sin would that be?" he asked silkily. "That of not obeying their husbands perhaps?" He hauled her into his arms and kissed her, his hands teasing her breasts through the thin fabric of her nightrail, weighing them, his thumbs circling the sensitive peaks until they hardened.

"You devil," she gasped breathlessly. "You know I cannot argue when you kiss me like that."

He laughed. "That is, obviously, the secret of marital accord." His eyes darkened. "I think a punishment for your disobedience is called for, and I must confess my first instinct was to put you across my knee."

Emily's mouth suddenly went dry. "And now?"

His eyes gleamed. "Now I have a much better idea. This punishment will prove to be a far more effective reminder to you. In fact, every time you look at me you will be reminded of it," he said softly. "And so will I." he added. "Now take off your nightrail."

Her eyes could not have been any bigger. "Take off my what?"

His grin was wolfish. "You heard me I think. Take of your nightrail or I will."

"Are you mad?"

"Only since I met you. Now, are you to take it off or shall I? I warn you I shall not waste my time with ribbons and ties."

A second later, the nightrail lay in a pool at her feet.

"Don't," he commanded as she tried to cover her nakedness with her hands. "I want to see you."

Emily thought Robert must be able to hear her heart beating, but she found she was not afraid, but excited. She stood straight. She would not cower in front of him.

Robert eyes feasted on the sight. He was the first and would be the only man to see her beautiful body—the unblemished skin, her rounded breasts, their pink tips pointing upwards, her narrow waist, and long, shapely legs dusted with fine hair at their juncture.

"My God, you are more beautiful even than I imagined."

"Well, have you seen your fill?" Her voice sounded husky.

Emily suddenly realised she wanted him to touch her. She wanted to feel his hands on her breasts and lower. She blushed as she realised she wanted him to touch her in that most secret of places. She felt herself growing wet.

"Oh, I have not seen my fill," he murmured. "I will never see my fill." He stepped forwards and swooped her into his arms, laying her on the bed. "I am going to pleasure you, Emily. I will not take your virginity, but at the end of this 'punishment,' you will be in no doubt as to who is your master."

"Master? You will be my husband, but you will not be—"

Her words were cut off as his lips took hers, urging her to open her mouth so his tongue could enter. When she stilled, he raised his mouth so that he could look in her eyes.

"No more arguments, my love, or I shall take the cords and tie you to the bed and my neck cloth will serve as a gag, though I do not want to gag you because I want to hear you cry out to me."

Emily paused. "In pain?" she said in a small voice.

"No, my love, in pleasure."

He dipped his head and traced a trail of kisses from her throat before taking the tip of one breast in his mouth. Emily moaned as he laved and swirled his tongue around, his hand giving equal attention to the other.

"Oh my," she gasped. He chuckled as his head slid lower, trailing kisses across her abdomen and stomach.

"Your Grace." Her words came on a strangled breath as he dipped his head still further.

"Open your legs for me," he said as he positioned himself.

"You cannot mean to…" She could not say it.

"Oh I fully intend to caress every single part of your body, my love."

When his tongue touched her, she acted purely instinctively, her hips raised of their own accord as his tongue slipped in and out of her in a slow, seductive rhythm. When he located the sensitive nub, his tongue gave it lavish attention until she thought she would faint.

Robert raised his head. "I want to see you come for me, Emily," he growled, desperately needing his own release, but he would not break his vow even though he knew Emily would not deny him.

Once they were married, he knew that sexually they would match. The woman writhing in pleasure was a sensual woman and he would enjoy teaching her what pleased him as well as learning what pleased her. Keeping his thumb on her bud, he slid two fingers into her warm wetness, easing them in and out and circling his thumb, watching her nipples tighten even further as her tension built. His fingers were relentless until he heard her cry his name and felt the waves of her pleasure. When she stilled, he drew her into his arms.

"Oh, Your Grace, Robert," she breathed in wonder. "I have never, I mean I didn't know... Is this the secret of the marriage bed?"

He smiled into her eyes. "One of them, my sweet."

Her eyes widened. "There is more?"

"There is much more. This is merely the first lesson.

"I think I may die of pleasure," she muttered.

"Remember that when you look at my lips. Remember the pleasure they can bring, and when our fingertips meet, remember what they can do to you."

His smile turned to a laugh. If it were possible, his delightfully wanton fiancée was blushing, all over. He looked forward to 'punishing' her again, even though he began to think that it might kill him.

Chapter Twenty-Eight

"What is this about a choir?" Lady Tremaine demanded as she swept into the breakfast room.

Robert looked up from his newspaper. "Emily has been rehearsing a choir. They performed last night at the Advent Service. They were a great success by all accounts."

"I should say so. I believe we are to receive several callers if the servants are to be believed."

Emily looked from one to the other. "But how? It was only one small choir in one small service. It was miles away and nowhere near anywhere fashionable."

"My dear, servants' gossip travels faster than the fire of London, and it seems that some of the ton were there to hear your choir. Apparently you are quite the talk of the town." Robert's mother was clearly intrigued. "It should make for a most interesting time tonight at the Gynn Masquerade. You must tell me everything, my dear, as we are about our shopping today. I should hate it if my friends thought they knew more than me."

"Just ensure Emily does not get into any more scrapes today, mother," Robert drawled as he handed the two women into the carriage, his fingers closing on Emily's hand. "We wouldn't wish to have to punish her again tonight," he murmured, his eyes gleaming.

Lady Tremaine had the whole story out of Emily before they had finished at the modiste who was making her wedding gown. "My, my. I must say Robert will have his hands more than full with you. That's exactly as it should be. Robert needs a wife who will challenge him so he does not get bored. I rather feel he has met his match. He may think he wants an obedient wife, but the reality is entirely different."

At the word obedient, Emily nearly choked. "He has made his thoughts on obedience quite clear, my lady."

Robert surprised them by joining them for the visiting hour. He frowned at the number of bouquets that had been delivered, catching Emily's hand as she handed him a cake. "These young men apparently do not know the rules. I shall have to call them all out."

"You cannot mean to fight a duel for the sake of a few flowers?" she gasped. "Apart from it being illegal, it is ridiculous."

"The rules are quite clear. By sending flowers to my affianced bride, they have insulted my honour. This must be restored by the fighting of a duel," he responded, but Emily noticed a gleam in his eye.

"Fighting duels insults my intelligence," Emily said.

"I'm afraid the feelings of the lady are not taken into account once the challenge has been made," he said loftily. He loved it when Emily got that look in her eye.

"Exactly," she replied crisply. "Because if they were, the concept of men fighting duels over some supposed slight is ridiculous?"

"How so?" He was intrigued.

"Well in the matter of honour, I cannot see how if my honour is compromised, you fighting another man will improve it. A person, male or female, is responsible for their own honour. According to your mother, if you fight a duel over me, my honour and reputation will be completely destroyed, so how does a duel protect it?"

"And if it is my honour?"

She raised an eyebrow. "How exactly is your honour restored by possibly killing another man? Is this an example of masculine logic? That a young man buys a few flowers for a woman and gets his head shot off? It seems rather an expensive price to pay."

Robert grinned. "Well since you put it so charmingly, at the Gynn Masquerade I'll content myself with glowering at any young buck who comes too close and content myself with knowing that although they may admire you from a distance, you are mine."

Emily rolled her eyes and shook her head, but she could not suppress a smile. Robert took a bite out of the cake.

As she was getting ready for the ball there was a knock at the door. Alice opened it and retrieved the message from a footman. When Emily saw the handwriting, she paled.

"Are you all right, Miss?" Alice looked concerned, "You've gone as white as a sheet."

"I'm fine, Alice. Would you fetch a little water, please?"

As soon as Alice left, Emily broke the seal and read her uncle's note.

Your family has taken too much from me already. I want what's mine.

She quickly folded the note and pushed it in a drawer. She had thought her uncle had given up hounding her and her betrothal to Robert had made her safe, but she was not. Her uncle was clearly a desperate man, and desperate men were likely to do desperate things.

Emily was in a quandary. She knew she should tell Robert about the note, but for all her uncle had done, she couldn't bring herself to hand him over to the authorities. In any case, what could she say? That he had arranged an unsuitable marriage—that happened to girls every day. That he had tried to cheat her out of her inheritance? She had no evidence, let alone proof. Nothing was written down. All he would say was that he had arranged her betrothal to a friend and every father in the ton would be on his side. She needed time to think.

By the time Alice returned with the glass of water, Emily had penned a quick note suggesting she would meet her uncle the following day. She needed to know what he planned to do, but one thing was certain, he would never have Ellerton.

Chapter Twenty-Nine

No one observing Emily Conrad at the Gynn Masquerade would have any idea that her life was less than perfect. She looked stunning in her disguise as a sea nymph, the green gown highlighting her creamy skin and titian hair, the mask adding a hint of mystery. She had been slightly shocked at the close fit of the gown, it clung to her like a second skin, the train floating behind like a tail.

Emily was grateful for the relative anonymity of the mask. As she danced, laughed, and spoke she felt like an automaton. All the time her mind worked on how she was going to deal with her uncle. The worse thing was that she didn't know how, when, or where he would contact her again. She didn't have to wait long.

During the supper interval she excused herself, saying she needed to go to the retiring room. As she walked back down the corridor she became aware of someone behind her. When she turned, a hand shot out and grabbed her arm while the other hand clamped over her mouth. Her assailant kicked the door open behind him and bundled her into the empty room.

It took several seconds for her eyes to adjust to the dim light. The man had not loosened his grip. She smelled leather, horses, and sweat from him and her own fear.

"I'm going to take my hand from your mouth, but if you struggle or scream, I shall bind and gag you." His face was close to hers but masked and hidden by shadows. His breath smelled of brandy. However, Emily did not need to see her attacker. She knew who he was.

She nodded her head and his grip relaxed. "What do you plan to do with me, uncle? Robert is downstairs. He will kill you for this."

Her uncle laughed, the sound humourless and bitter. "You don't need to know my plans for you, but know this, at this very moment some of my men are in the supper room, one is standing not two feet away from your fiancé. If they receive my signal within the next few minutes, one will create a diversion and the other will plunge a dagger into the Duke of Whitney's heart. If you do not do exactly as I say, I will give that signal. Do you understand?"

Emily's eyes widened in horror. She had no doubt her uncle was mad and possibly desperate enough to try anything, but to have Robert murdered? "I don't believe you, uncle. Surely you would never do such a thing."

He laughed again. "My dear niece, you have no idea of what I am capable if the need arises. In any case," he added, his eyes boring into hers, "can you afford to risk it?"

Emily didn't hesitate. "No." She would do what she had to save Robert. "I'll do as you ask, just don't harm him." Try as she might to keep her voice strong, the words came out as a sob.

His grip relaxed a little more. "Good, I'm glad you're being sensible. Get your cloak and pull the hood down low. You and I are going to leave as though there is nothing amiss. Do you understand?" She nodded,

"Robert will come after me."

Her uncle smiled. "I think not, my dear. He has been given a message from you saying you are feeling unwell and have gone home and you will see him in the morning. You are such an amiable fiancée that you told him to go to his club and enjoy the rest of his evening."

She left the house with her heart growing heavier with every step. Her uncle had clearly been planning her abduction for some time and had thought of everything. She was bundled into an unmarked coach, the leather curtains drawn down so she had no idea in which direction she was going.

"Could I not stop by the house to change my clothing. This is hardly suitable attire for travelling?" If she could persuade her uncle to stop off at the house she might be able to get a message to Robert somehow.

"No need..." he grunted. You will be provided with all you need when we reach our destination."

"But—"

"Either be quiet or I shall gag you," he threatened.

Confident Emily would obey, he closed his eyes and within minutes started to snore. The coach jolted and rattled as it tore through London. Every so often the leather curtain would lift, but it was dark and Emily could not tell where she was, though after a while, the frantic pace lessened, and she began to think they had left London behind and were travelling on a country road. As the coach slowed, she began to wonder if she could somehow open the door and jump out before her uncle woke. She began to edge towards the door and quietly reached her hand out towards the handle, keeping her eyes on her uncle. His eyes remained closed. As her hand closed on the handle she screamed as his hand shot out and grasped her wrist.

"Foolish girl, now I shall have to bind you." Before she had time to react he wrapped her wrists with stout rope. "Now are you going to keep your mouth closed or do I have to gag you?"

Eyes wide with fear, she shook her head. Emily was beyond shocked. She had not realised the depths to which her uncle had sunk. It was not just the money, though clearly he had need of it. His greatcoat was frayed and the cuffs caked in dirt. The rage he felt towards the family whom he perceived had cheated him out of what was rightfully his frightened her.

For almost a year she had not heard from him. Hidden away, he must have nursed his resentment until now, days before her wedding, he acted. She could not help the sob that escaped her throat. Once she was married, he would no longer be eligible to inherit her estate. She now knew what fate lay in store for her. Her uncle intended to kill her or have her killed before her wedding.

The man opposite looked at her with a mixture of revulsion and pleasure. "I warned you to be quiet, Miss, but like your mother, you just could not do as you were told." He ripped the hem of her dress and tied it firmly around her mouth. "Don't imagine your lover will come to your rescue. He will never find you, no-one will." He laughed, watching her face as she digested his words. "Now, Miss, if you have any sense, any sense whatsoever, you'll do exactly as I say."

After a few hours in the carriage, Emily had no idea where she was.

They stopped only to change horses and take food, though she could eat nothing. They halted briefly for personal needs but even then, her uncle merely turned his back and there was no chance of escape. When she climbed back into the coach, he grunted.

"Get some sleep. We've a long way to go yet."

She did not think she would be able to sleep but exhaustion finally overcame her. When she woke the carriage had stopped. The air was considerably cooler and she shivered, but whether it was from cold or fear she could not determine.

Her uncle dragged her from the carriage. Although it was dark, there was enough moonlight for her to make out a small cottage. Her uncle kicked the door open and shoved her inside.

Once he lit a candle, she could see the cottage had not been lived in for some time. The dusty hearth revealed a fire had been laid. A wooden table held a few more candles, a jug of water, a loaf of bread, and some cheese.

"There's a bed through there." Her uncle nodded to a curtain hanging on the wall. "I'll release your hands now because I'll be locking the door and one of my men will be guarding it." He cut her bonds with a knife. "Don't think of doing anything you might regret," he warned before slamming the door shut behind him. She heard the sound of a bolt being driven home on the outside.

Emily stood rubbing some feeling back into her wrists. Clearly her uncle didn't intend to kill her immediately. Behind the curtain was an alcove with a small bed and some of her old clothes from Ellerton. It seemed her uncle had been planning this carefully. She quickly changed into the clothes. They were warmer and more practical than the mermaid gown. There was no other room. The shutters at the windows had been nailed shut—not that she would have known where to go if she could manage to escape. She could not be at Ellerton because she knew every cottage there. So, where was she?

Chapter Thirty

"Where the hell is she?" Robert shouted.

He was not a man to lose his temper. Even in the thick of battle he was renowned for keeping a cool, clear head. However, the discovery that Emily was missing made fear race through his mind.

"She sent me a message she was feeling unwell and that I was to continue the evening without her," he said. When I rose this morning, I find her maid in tears because she had been sent a message to say she was not needed and could go to bed. Emily is missing, apparently not having been home at all."

"If we could remain calm, Your Grace," Burrows began. "I have men already searching—"

"Keep calm? I'll remind you, Burrows, the last time she disappeared it took months to find her."

"The last time, Sir, Miss Conrad did not want to be found," Burrows reminded him calmly. "It appears Miss Conrad was escorted from the Ball by a man."

"What?"

"One of Lady Gynn's footmen saw Miss Conrad being led away by a man whom he described as a large older gentleman in a long cloak.

"Her uncle, it has to be."

"Sir Clifford is not at Ellerton. My men have already checked."

"Then where the hell is he? I should have had him watched." Robert paced. "I knew I shouldn't have trusted him. He needs money, Burrows, desperately, and he sees Miss Conrad as the way to get it."

Burrows looked up from the note he was reading. "You think he has abducted Miss Conrad to extort a ransom from you."

Robert poured himself a generous measure of brandy and tossed it down. "If only it were that simple." He sat down behind the desk in an attempt to calm himself.

"Apparently Emily is a wealthy young woman. She inherited both from her parents and her grandmother, but in an attempt to ensure the money was not accessed by that profligate, it was tied up in trusts." He ran a hand through his hair. "Miss Conrad should have been able to access the money, but somehow he managed to gain control of her solicitor and kept the money from her so she could barely keep the estate and the house going. He planned to pressure her into marrying one of his cronies, who would gain control of her money. I assume they planned to split the money between them."

Burrows steepled his fingers as he digested the information. "But surely all he had to do was to have her killed. Then he would have inherited it all."

Robert's face paled. The thought of Emily being harmed filled him with the kind of fear he had never felt before. It was several minutes before he could bring himself to reply.

"I can only assume that, blackguard though he is, Hammond is no murderer."

"Perhaps he has not yet had the right opportunity," Burrows replied. "He would have to plan so he was beyond suspicion."

Robert looked at Burrows with distaste. "This is my fiancée you are talking about. Have a care."

Burrows did not flinch from the Duke's stare. "I am merely considering all possible avenues of investigation, Your Grace. I apologise if I have offended you."

Robert dropped his head in his hands. "No, Burrows, you are quite right to consider all possibilities, even those of which I cannot bear to think."

The door opened. James, followed by and his mother, entered. It was clear Lady Tremaine had been crying.

"Robert, I have just heard about Emily. What's to be done? Surely you have men out looking for her. She cannot have gone far." The words tumbled from his mother's mouth.

Robert sighed, deciding she should know the situation fully. "I have men out looking, but the villains had many hours start on us. She and her uncle seem to have disappeared from the face of the earth. James, ring for Hunter to bring tea for mother."

Lady Tremaine sat on the sofa. "I do not need tea, Robert." She fixed him with a steely glance. "I need a brandy."

Despite the seriousness of the situation, both brothers smiled. If the soldiers of the British army were respected and feared by their enemies, they would turn to jelly when faced with formidable British women.

Lady Tremaine took more than a ladylike sip and set the glass down. "Now tell me what has been done and what the plan is."

Half an hour later, she shook her head thoughtfully. "So, if I have this right, you think Sir Clifford abducted Emily from the Gynn Masquerade last night, and we know he is not at Ellerton Grange."

"My men have thoroughly searched the house and all the outbuildings as well as the estate," Burrows said. "According to his servants, he hasn't been at Ellerton for some months."

"And he's not at the town house?" She took another sip of brandy.

"He hasn't used the town house for a long time. It's let to Sir Anthony Hutchinson. He's taken it for the last three seasons for his daughters' coming out," Burrows replied.

"And they have no other estate? No hunting lodge?"

Robert was impressed. Both his mother and Emily had made him reconsider the intellectual properties of women. He would be mindful in future to ensure he listened to what they had to say.

"There was an estate in the north," Burrows began, "However, I don't believe it has been used for years. The moors have probably reclaimed it by now. It's quite far north I believe."

Robert took a sharp intake of breath. "I'll bet that's where the old dog has taken her. Fetch me a map."

Within moments the large map was laid out on the desk with the three men and Lady Tremaine studying it intently. "That's it," Robert pointed. "All of that is the Conrad estate."

"But why did Sir Clifford keep this from Emily? She was under the impression the only thing in her possession was Ellerton Grange and that there was insufficient money to maintain it," James said.

"Sir Clifford was clearly in league with that crooked lawyer. Somehow they managed to keep Emily ignorant of quite how much she owned so they could manipulate her into marrying someone they could either also control or who had agreed to share the money between them," Burrows explained.

"Cropton?"

The investigator pointed to the map. "Whose estate borders Conrad land, here?"

"Cropton." Both brothers spoke at once.

"Of course, how could I have not seen this?" Robert growled. "Emily's uncle and Cropton have been in league all along. Cropton was to marry Emily and they planned to split her money between them, presumably with the lawyer getting a cut. When Emily thwarted their plans by running away, they had to think of something else. The fact that Emily became betrothed to me has made them desperate."

"Cropton is in debt up to his eyeballs," James added. "He's either mortgaged or sold virtually all he inherited. His creditors are getting impatient. I believe he's ruined."

"Forgive me, Your Grace, but I am still puzzled as to why Sir Clifford just didn't arrange for his niece to have some kind of accident. It would have been fairly simple to accomplish, and he would have been left with the complete inheritance without having to share with the lawyer or Cropton." Burrows frowned.

"I should imagine both the lawyer and Sir Richard have some hold over him." Lady Tremaine sipped her brandy. "Perhaps all three know something scandalous, not to say criminal about the others, so as long as they work together they are all safe. Then again, I am only a woman. What do I know about the workings of the criminal world?" She took another sip of her brandy.

Robert crossed to where she sat on the sofa and dropped a kiss on her head. "Never again let it be said that you are 'just a woman,' mother. I think you have worked out their scheming."

He strode to the door. "James, Burrows, there is no time to delay. Emily is in danger. Once she is married to Cropton, she is of no further use to either of them."

Chapter Thirty-One

Emily reckoned she had been in the cottage for a week. During that time, she had seen no one other than the guards outside and the woman who brought her a basket of food. Of her uncle, she had seen nothing.

She had swept the cottage. Never one to sit still for too long, she would go mad without employment of some kind, so she changed into the plain gown and apron then swept and dusted the dirt and cobwebs away. Activity helped to take her mind off her situation. She believed Robert would move heaven and earth to find her. She had to believe that, but what if he could not? What if he believed the lies her uncle had spread about her? He had forgiven her once, but would he do it again?

The cottage door stood slightly open as she approached it. After a few days of carrying her water from the well, the guard allowed her to go the well on her own. Emily did not mind fetching her own water and was glad of the opportunity to go outside, even if it was only to the bottom of the garden.

"You've a visitor," the guard said as he pushed the door fully open and then closed it as she went inside.

Sitting on the Windsor chair, with his booted feet on the hearth was Sir Richard Cropton. "So, enjoying playing the part of the country maid?" he drawled.

"I have little choice," she replied. Although she was determined not to show her fear, the hairs on the back of her neck rose. Sir Richard was dangerous, unpredictable, and not only did he despise all women, he despised her in particular, especially since she had rejected his previous advances.

"Well, I must admit when Clifford told me of his plan to abduct you, I didn't think he had a hope in hell of carrying it off, but here we are, my dear. About to become man and wife once again."

Emily stared at the floor.

"What? Don't tell me the vociferous Miss Emily has nothing to say. I must confess I find that hard to believe." His voice was smooth as silk. Emily said nothing.

"Come here," he commanded. Emily glanced at the door.

Sir Richard laughed. "The guard is one of my men. Now come here. I shall not ask again." Emily stood in front of him.

He rose. "Look at me." He tapped his riding crop lightly against his thigh as he waited for her to obey. After a few seconds, he placed it under her chin, forcing her head back, his eyes glittering.

"When we last met, I was disappointed our relationship got off to a poor start, so I shall make it clear to you now what I expect. As my wife, you will come to me whenever you are required. I shall have you when I want, where I want, and how I want." He stepped closer. "I have many and varied tastes which you will learn to accept. I will do things to you that you cannot even begin to imagine, my dear, and I shall enjoy them. Intensely. Your sole purpose will be to please and pleasure me. Do you understand?"

The tension on her neck increased. When she did not reply he pushed the crop higher.

"Do you understand?" he repeated softly.

"Yes," she whispered.

"I didn't hear you, say it again." Another push.

"Yes, I understand." Her voice was calm, but inside she was shaking.

Emily had been wary of Sir Richard from the outset, but only now was the depth of his depravity clear. He abruptly released her and walked behind her, placing his hands lightly on her shoulders. Emily fought to stop herself from flinching at his touch.

"Ah, my dear," he breathed into her ear. "I begin to think we might suit after all." He pulled her sleeve from her shoulder and lightly grazed her skin with his fingers.

He laughed. "Yes, we shall suit well, now that you know something of my expectations." His breath felt warm against her skin. "If you do not please me…well we shall see."

He walked around her once again. "I have a desire to see what I am getting for my bride."

Before she knew what was happening, he had ripped the bodice of her gown. Her thin chemise was all that remained between him and her nakedness.

He licked his lips. "You have grown into quite a woman, Lady Emily." He reached for her and she resisted.

The door crashed open as they struggled and her uncle burst into the room. For the first time in her life, Emily was glad to see him.

"Cropton, what the hell do you think you're doing? Take your hands off my niece."

Sir Richard took a step back and leaned against the table, tapping his crop against his breeches. "I was merely inspecting the goods. I fail to see what the problem is. In a few days she will be mine to deal with as I see fit. If I choose to keep her naked and chained to a bed, it will be my right," he drawled. "Rather a delightful prospect I must admit."

"When you are her husband, you will be responsible for her, but until then, she shall remain innocent."

Cropton gave an ironic bow. "As you wish. I suppose a few more days wait will make the fruit more ripe and sweet." He forced her chin up with his crop. "You know what waits." His eyes bored into hers.

As he headed towards the door, Sir Clifford caught his arm. "You will treat her well."

Sir Richard shrugged him off. "It's a little too late to play the concerned guardian don't you think?"

Chapter Thirty-Two

Sir Clifford helped Emily to her feet. "I apologise, my dear. I had no idea Sir Richard would come to the cottage. Here." He offered Emily his hip flask. "Drink this, it will calm you."

Like a puppet, Emily did as she was bid, coughing as the brandy hit the back of her throat. She pulled the sides of her bodice together as best she could. The fear she felt at the hands of Sir Richard was replaced by anger.

"Why are you doing this to me, uncle? Surely you know what kind of man Sir Richard is." If her bodice hung open, she didn't care she decided. Let him see the sort of man with whom they were dealing.

Sir Clifford took a quick nip of brandy before he replied. "Cropton and I were at school together. He's the only one of my friends who stood by me when my inheritance was denied me."

"Not to mention the fact that when he gains control of my money, he has promised to share it with you." Emily's voice dripped with contempt. Her uncle had the grace to blush at her words.

"How do you know Sir Richard will keep to his side of the bargain? Once I am married off to him, he might choose to keep the money for himself."

"Cropton would never double deal. He's a friend," Sir Clifford protested, but Emily could see from the look in his eyes that her words had unsettled him.

"Friend? What sort of a friend is he that will marry just for money? I know he means to make my life a living hell if this wedding happens."

Sir Clifford collected himself. "This wedding will happen and within two days. You must accustom yourself to the notion and not behave in your usual headstrong manner."

"You should have just killed me, uncle. It would have been less trouble."

Sir Clifford looked genuinely shocked at her words. "I couldn't do that, my dear."

"At least it would have been quick. You would condemn me instead to a man whose only interest is to harass and punish me for the rest of my life. I would rather be dead than marry a man whom I could never love."

Her eyes swam with tears as she thought for a moment of Robert, the man she loved with all her heart and whom she could now never have. Even if by some miracle she didn't marry Sir Richard Cropton, she would be so tarnished by this hideous experience that she could never be received by society, not even with her handsome duke by her side.

Sir Clifford's eyes hardened. "Love? Your parents married for love and much good it did them. Marriage is nothing to do with love. If you expected love, you should have been born a peasant."

"But you saw what he did to me, uncle," she cried.

"How a man treats his wife is his own affair."

"Uncle, surely you must know, friend or no, Sir Richard does not behave like a normal man nor would he behave like a normal husband. There is a streak of cruelty to him you cannot have missed. He takes spiteful pleasure in intimidating and hurting others."

"As a boy he was always pulling the wings from moths and tying things to the tails of cats and dogs to make them mad," Sir Clifford admitted.

"There, and as a man he has not changed. Now his targets are bigger and his torments larger." Emily held her breath as Sir Clifford paused.

"A few stupid tricks as a boy have nothing to do with this. In any case, it's too late. You will marry Sir Richard and there's an end to it." Emily sank to the floor.

"You must accustom yourself to your new situation. Please Sir Richard and he will treat you kindly, of that I am sure. Give him an heir and he will lose interest in you completely. He has learned that on the birth of his heir he will receive an endowment, so an heir is imperative," he explained.

"Sir Richard should never be allowed within ten miles of any child," Emily shot back. "He is a libertine, a cad, and I have no doubt would torment his child as much as he torments everyone else." Emily could not disguise the revulsion she felt.

Her uncle patted her shoulder. "Once the child is born, you need not fear. I doubt either of you would see Sir Richard. He will have his endowment and your fortune and will leave you alone up here while he continues his life in London."

Emily shook free of her uncle's hand. "You think that's all right, do you, uncle? You sell me in marriage to a man I detest and who I am pretty sure detests me. I am to give him an heir and then be shut away up here for the rest of my life. Why didn't you just kill me because that's what you're doing. However, instead of doing it in one swift movement, you're doing it like slow acting poison."

Her uncle stood up and put on his hat. "Emily, the marriage will take place, and you must make of it what you will. The next time I see you will be at the church. Then you and I will be free of each other."

Emily stood, glaring into his eyes. "When Robert hears of this he will kill you."

Sir Clifford paused in mid stride. "The Duke of Whitney has no idea where you are, my dear. So, if you have some notion he will come riding to your rescue, forget it."

"Do you have no feeling for me at all, uncle?"

"It's nothing personal. I need the money and you are the only way I have of raising it." He closed the door quietly.

Robert would come. He must.

Chapter Thirty-Three

Robert paced the room. They had pressed on as far as they could before nightfall when James had persuaded Robert they must stop.

"Fresh horses and fresh senses will serve to rescue Emily better than jaded horses and tired men," he said, and though Robert wanted to get to Emily as soon as possible, he had to agree.

The inn was small but only twenty miles short of the estate. One thing was clear from the landlord, Sir Richard Cropton was disliked by his tenants and workers alike. He could not bear the thought of Emily's suffering and vowed that when he found her, he would never leave her side.

He was afraid they would fail. The Cropton estate was large, though neglected, but there were plenty of buildings on it where Emily could be hidden. Worse, while they were searching, Cropton and her uncle would have the time to spirit her away again. He leaned his head on his arm as he paused his pacing and stood in front of the fireplace. All he had brought Emily was trouble and unhappiness. When he rescued her, she would be within her rights to want nothing more to do with him. That was true of all the men with whom she had come into contact.

He could not blame her if, once she had control of her fortune, she wanted nothing more to do with any of them. Yet, he could not believe that. The force of his love for her would not let her waste her life alone. She should be surrounded with love, his love, and in time, that of their family. He could not lose her now.

The door opened and James entered carrying a flagon of wine.

"Come, brother, you look like you need some of this," he said pouring out two generous glasses. "For the first time on this mission, I have some good news." He sat down and took a drink.

Robert sat with him, "What? What news?"

"There are a couple of local lads downstairs. I bought them a few drinks and they were quite free with their tongues. They have been guarding a young woman."

Silence reigned while Robert digested the information. He sprang to his feet. "Come, we must go at once."

"Steady, brother, Miss Conrad is being held in a cottage in the heart of the estate. We'd never get to her before they moved her. No, there's a much better way of reaching her." He took another sip. "Burrows has just sent a message. He tracked down Hook, the lawyer."

Robert's eyebrows rose. "And?"

James grinned. "Once Burrows had a word, Hook was only too happy to talk. It seems he regretted his actions regarding Emily, especially when Burrows pointed out these actions were enough to get him imprisoned for a very long time. It seems Hook is not a great lawyer. There are several of his clients who would welcome him into prison, if you catch my meaning."

Robert could feel himself grinding his teeth in impatience. "What did he say about Emily now? We can deal with the rest of his misdeeds when we've rescued her."

James leaned forward. "That's the interesting part. Hook knows all about the plan because he was to have a share of the spoils as we thought. Emily is being kept in a cottage on the estate, but in two days time is to be wed to Sir Richard Cropton at the chapel on the estate."

Robert surged to his feet. "The hell she is!" he shouted.

"That's where Hook's information is invaluable. We can get our men in position near the chapel, stop the wedding, and we'll be able to capture Sir Clifford and Sir Richard at the same time," James explained. "Believe me, the chapel is far easier to find than any one of the cottages where she could be held," he added.

"What about Sir Richard's men? Won't the estate be swarming with them?" Robert frowned.

"That's where buying a few drinks for the men downstairs was a good investment. They have no loyalty to Sir Richard. His tenants complain that he raises the rents but does nothing to support them. He has not paid his men for a month and treats them like dogs. A little silver will secure their co-operation."

Robert jumped to his feet. "Go back to the men and tell them any man who wants to join us should be here to be paid at first light tomorrow. Burrows is on his way. If we can achieve Emily's release without cracking skulls, so much the better. Whatever we do, we must make sure we do not put Emily in further danger. If one of the men seems like a leader, we'll need to speak to him. He will be able to help us plan our strategy."

Chapter Thirty-Four

The glass reflected Emily's pale face as she looked at herself in the mirror. Her uncle had sent over wedding clothes, a veil, and a woman from the house to help her dress. Silent tears coursed down her cheeks as the woman fixed orange blossom in her hair. It was really happening. In a few short hours she would be married to Sir Richard Cropton. There would be no rescue. Robert had not come. The woman made no comment, apart from telling Emily that her uncle had sent her, she said not a word.

Emily heard the rumble of wheels and horses stop outside the door. Her uncle entered. For once he had made an effort. In anticipation of the money that would shortly be coming his way, he was dressed in a new peacock blue coat and breeches with a gold waistcoat. His hair had been freshly dressed and there was a distinct spring in his step.

"Come, my dear. You look quite beautiful. We must not keep your bridegroom waiting. Sir Richard is already at the chapel and eager to get on with it."

"The wedding or spending my money?" Emily said wryly.

"Now, we'll have none of that, my lady. It is your wedding day."

It was not the wedding day Emily had anticipated. She had thought about trying to run away at the last moment, but she knew it was hopeless. She would be recaptured before she had run a few feet, quite apart from the fact that she would not even be able to find her way off the estate. Her only chance was to go through with this farce of a wedding and hope she could escape later when Sir Richard and her uncle were well in their cups, which she had no doubt would happen after the ceremony. She had already discounted appealing to the vicar who was no doubt in the pay of the Cropton family.

"I am glad you have accepted your situation," Sir Clifford remarked as he handed her into the carriage. "It is always wise to make the best of these things." Emily said nothing.

"Here, I brought these for you." He produced a small bouquet. "A bride should have flowers."

"Thank you." Emily took the flowers and placed them on the seat. It was as though her uncle was now convinced that this was a proper wedding.

Within minutes they arrived at the small chapel. There was no music, no flowers, no guests. Sir Richard stood at the front with the vicar. Sir Clifford and another man she did not recognise were to stand as witnesses.

"Dearly beloved," the vicar intoned.

"Just get on with it man," Sir Richard snapped. "Get to the pronouncement then we can be done with this. There is no one to know or care whether the words have been spoken or not."

"I must say the words, Sir, or it is not a legal marriage," the vicar stammered.

"Very well, but get a move on."

"Dearly beloved," the vicar began again, though noticeably quicker. As the words washed over her, Emily barely noticed them until the door crashed open. Within seconds Robert strode down the aisle with James and other men slightly behind them.

"Make the pronouncement now, damn you," Sir Richard hissed, grabbing Emily's arm and pulling her towards him.

"You're too late, Your Grace," he sneered. "The lady is married to me in the sight of God and man. May I present the new Lady Cropton."

"The hell she is," Robert growled. "The lady was marrying you under duress. This wedding is nothing more than a farce. Now take your hands off my fiancée."

A moment's silence followed while Sir Richard considered his options. "I don't believe I will, Whitney. If I can't have her, then no one shall. Without her money, I am ruined anyway."

Robert stared horrified at the glitter of a blade now inches from Emily's throat.

"Cropton, what the devil are you doing?" Shock filled Sir Clifford's voice. "You promised not to harm her."

Sir Richard turned to his former friend with contempt etched in his face. "As my wife she had some value. Now she is worth nothing to me. I am ruined, and if I have to face the ignominy of the hangman or transportation, then I shall do so at least knowing my name will be remembered for something spectacular."

Throughout his speech, unnoticed by Sir Richard, Emily had been slowly moving her arm forward. There would be no reasoning with Sir Richard. He was quite mad. Robert would not attack for fear of harming her. She knew if she was to be saved, she must do it herself.

"Sir Richard," she said softly, before bringing her elbow sharply into his ribs. It was enough to surprise him into dropping the knife, which she kicked away.

"You little bitch!" he yelled, grabbing for her again.

This time Emily was determined not to allow herself to be caught. Instinctively she brought her other arm up and punched him in the face, hearing a crack as she made contact with his nose.

Within seconds, Sir Richard was on the floor, trussed like a turkey. Robert's men had moved from the side aisle and secured him. In the next second, Emily was in Robert's arms.

"Thank God you're safe, my love, I have been going out of my mind with worry." He groaned. "I was afraid I had lost you a second time."

"You are certainly most lax where your fiancée is concerned. To lose me once was bad enough, but twice?" she teased, though shaking with relief, thinking of how close her uncle and Sir Richard had come to fulfilling their plan.

Robert looked down at her. "You are all right? That bastard didn't harm you?"

"No, my love. I think he intended to spend our marriage doing that."

Robert's eyes turned black. "Killing him would be a pleasure. He deserves nothing less."

"But not by you, let justice take its course. I fear he is one who will never choose to reform."

Robert turned to James. "Have Sir Richard locked up until he can be taken to the magistrate. Let the vicar go. He looks as though he's about to collapse. The magistrate can question him later."

"Emmy, I am so sorry. I had no idea Cropton was such a blackguard." Her uncle stood before them. "I thought that once he married you and you gave him an heir, he would treat you kindly, truly I did."

Emily stepped forward. "Uncle, one day I may be able to forgive you for the heartache you have caused, but for now I wish never to see you again. All you have done is to plot and plan how to get your hands on my fortune for your own good. You are my only relative and I would have loved you, but I see now that all I was for you was a purse."

Sir Clifford sighed. "What you say is true, but I will regret my actions for the rest of my life in the hope that one day you will find it in your heart to forgive me."

"Take him and the lawyer away, James, and see to it they are kept secure for the magistrate." Robert could not hide the disgust he felt for the older man and did not bother to try. He could hang for his part in this plot and, in all honesty, he should.

As they walked back down the aisle, Robert's arm firmly around Emily's waist, he began to relax for what felt like the first time since Emily had been abducted.

She looked up at him. "What does that smile mean?"

"I was just thinking that should we at any time argue during our marriage, I had best not allow you to become acquainted with a certain Gentleman Jackson. Your left hook is quite vicious enough as it is."

Chapter Thirty-Five

As she stood at the entrance to the church, Emily could not help but remember that a year ago she had landed unceremoniously at the feet of Robert, Duke of Whitney. Now, on Christmas Eve she was about to marry her handsome duke. The year had been tumultuous, from being accused of stealing diamonds, to training her choir, from entering society to being abducted. Since she had met Robert her life had been anything but dull and now she was about to take the most exciting step of her life.

The church looked magnificent. Garlands of evergreens adorned the ends of the pews, the pulpit, and the lectern, and it was lit by what seemed like a thousand candles, glowing and flickering, reflecting off the silver plate and stained glass. The dressmaker made a final adjustment to her veil, making sure the garland of white roses was secure. Lady Tremaine had offered her the suite of Whitney diamonds, including the fabulous tiara said to have once been owned by the Empress of Russia, but Emily had refused.

She wanted to come to Robert as herself. For so much of her life she had believed she had nothing because her uncle had kept her in ignorance of her fortune. When she had met Robert, he had fallen in love with her for herself and she wanted to remind him of that fact. Though she had no doubt that when he made her his Duchess he would enjoy ensuring she was as bejewelled as the rest of society.

"Are you ready?" James tucked her hand into the crook of his arm. It was his proud duty, in the absence of any male relatives, to give Emily away.

"I think so," she replied.

"Don't be nervous." He smiled to reassure her. "After all you have been through, especially in the last few days, this should be a pleasure."

"I don't want to let Robert down," she admitted. "I have not been born to this. What if I get it wrong? My uncle's actions have almost put me beyond the pale as it is. What if Robert regrets marrying beneath him?"

James patted her arm. "You have certainly chosen an interesting moment to voice your doubts, but let me set your mind at ease. My brother loves you, Emily. I have never seen him happier or more at peace. When you were missing, he nearly went out of his mind. I have never known a man so in love, and consider this," he went on, "you have had your trials and tribulations in the last year and have survived. If your love can survive that, it can survive anything."

"But what of society? Will they be so forgiving?" She bit her lip.

"Look inside the church. Were you to be the pariah you think, they would have stayed away."

Emily peeped through the doorway. The church was packed. All of society had turned out to see the Duke of Whitney married. From the strictest society ladies to some of her choir, Robert had invited them all, and they had come. Suddenly, the organ swelled and she found herself floating down the aisle to marry her handsome Duke.

Hours later, Robert tugged at Emily's sleeve. He had made polite conversation with the doughty matrons of the ton, watched as his bride danced with just about every man at their wedding, and smiled through endless pieces of advice from all the married men at the wedding. Now he had had enough. Although he wanted Emily to enjoy her wedding, there was nothing more he wanted than to take her upstairs and make love to her, something he had been aching to do since he had brought her back from Sir Richard Copton's estate.

"Come, Emily," he said quietly. "It's time."

"But what about our guests?"

"They won't miss us in the slightest. There is music, dancing, and enough food and drink to keep them happy for a week." He laughed before his face became mock serious. "Besides, now that you have finally promised to obey me, I want you naked and in my bed—now."

"Robert," Emily gasped, both shocked and excited. "You shouldn't say such things. What if someone heard?"

He laughed. "What if they did? I want the world to know I am in love with my wife, body and soul."

She looked up at him. "I like the sound of that."

Within moments, she had gone and within five minutes he had followed her, finding her exactly as he wanted, naked and in his bed.

* * * *

"Did you see that?" the Dowager Duchess of Crookham said to Lady Tremaine, her oldest friend. "Whitney and his new bride disappeared up the stairs not five minutes ago without so much as a by your leave."

"So I did." Lady Tremaine beamed. "I believe they have gone to view the wedding gifts."

"Wedding gifts, my foot," the dowager cackled. The only gift I imagine Whitney is interested in unwrapping is his wife.

She was right.

About the Author

Anna lives in a lovely village in Hampshire England with her own romantic hero, otherwise known as her long-suffering husband and has two grown up children. An ex-teacher, she has taught many subjects from religion to drama but has always had a passion for history and would love a time machine to experience life in Georgian England, though suspects she would have been one of the maids washing the cups rather than delicately sipping tea from them.

When she's not thinking about life in the nineteenth century, she enjoys travelling and learning about different customs and cultures, especially the food. Anna also loves to walk in the beautiful Yorkshire Dales which provides much inspiration for her writing. She also plays the piano and it's her ambition to be able to play well enough so that the cat doesn't leave the room.

Anna comes from a long tradition of women who love Christmas and enjoys hosting her family every year with lots of food, games and laughter so what better setting for romance.

21047670R00110

Printed in Poland
by Amazon Fulfillment
Poland Sp. z o.o., Wrocław